Scar Tissue

For Enge, with love

Scar Tissue

Clare Morgan

SEREN

Seren is the book imprint of
Poetry Wales Press Ltd,
4 Derwen Road, Bridgend, Wales, CF31 1LH

www.serenbooks.com
facebook.com/SerenBooks
Twitter: @SerenBooks

ISBN: 9781781726891
Ebook: 9781781726914

A CIP record for this title is available from the British Library.

The publisher acknowledges the financial assistance
of the Books Council of Wales.

Cover artwork: 'Ffigwr a Coeden' by Meirion Ginsberg.
Photograph courtesy of the Martin Tinney Gallery.

Printed by Severn, Gloucester

CONTENTS

1. SPACE

BREATHING ON THE MOON

Her feet are tender, and she never deigns
To set them on the earth, but softly steps
Upon the heads of men.

Plato, The Symposium

It was entirely because of Henry Miller that I came so early to be what you might call corrupt.

I didn't start off with the character of a female adventurer. Nothing, you understand, in the style of Henry himself in *Tropic of Capricorn*, fucking his way through the universe, proselytizing about redemption on the indrawn breath while he lifts his head from between a pair of spread legs.

I first read Henry when he got unbanned, a cheap-looking American edition, originally $7.50, reduced (because of popular demand) to 95c. The paper was rough to the touch and the print too crowded, so that the letters and the words were constantly jostling one another in a way that made you feel sea-sick, and the text was in perpetual danger of dropping off the page.

It went yellow very quickly, that 95c edition, and then before too long around the outside edges especially the yellow turned to a fragile-looking brown. But you could still make out the words, they were clear enough, and I turned to it often as I was growing up, so that I would know about these things, love, men and women, the way people are to one another. Usage, bondage, subservience and need. It was because of Henry Miller that I got to know so early what other people didn't seem to know.

Good old Henry.

My father was a Brooklyn Jew, so every time I read the word 'kike' it gave me a particular thrill. *Kike*, I thought, *kike*. Did it mean that I was one? My father had died when I was very little. He drove a yellow cab so my mother told me, and was out until all hours trying to get fares.

A good man, my mother would tell me sometimes. But no job for a man with a family. What kind of life did we have, I ask you? No life.

My mother was not Jewish, but she had lived with my father for a long time, so she sometimes sounded like a Jew. The more Jewish she sounded, the more her mouth moved. I wondered whether my father's mouth had moved like that. I had a photograph of him, but his mouth was in a line with his lips closed.

He died, so the story went, of a heart attack, at one o'clock in the morning.

Thank God he wasn't driving! my mother often said, even years afterwards, breathing very heavily and clasping, with a fine dramatic emphasis, her hands.

Thank God he had stopped for a fare.

My father died, so she told me, leaning across the passenger seat of his yellow cab, as though he was just about to open the door.

I thought what a fright he must have given his prospective passenger as his face contorted and he clawed at the air. Maybe it was that act of leaning forwards, doubling his heart up against his belly, congesting everything, that finally did him in.

He was very careful with himself, my mother often said. He knew, if you ask me.

I didn't ask her, but she kept on telling me. All my growing up years were infused with the aura of my increasingly long dead father.

On the anniversary of that wet night when he leaned across the inside of his cab and something finally burst inside him, there was always lamentation, and an atmosphere. As I got older it occurred to me that the atmosphere was somehow manufactured. People, my mother even, seemed to have to *try* so hard at their grief. I've always found that grief is something inside you. The more you show it, the more adulterated it becomes. I think grief should be pure, as pure as you can make it. I think everything you feel should be pure, I mean, clean and sharp, like a knife when it cuts you, as separate from every other feeling as it can be.

I began reading *Tropic of Capricorn* on the day they launched Yuri Gagarin into those realms that neither man nor God can stake a claim to.

Space, we call it, that cold zone of nothingness from which we came and to which we will return inevitably.

I had looked at the sky every night in the previous week with a diligence that was not habitual.

Come away from the window, my mother said, It is past your bed-time.

My grandmother had died and I thought I might see her soul, or some sign of it, up where the stars were, for that is where souls went.

Did my grandmother and Yuri Gagarin pass one another like passengers riding in different time frames?

I asked this of my mother but she did not respond to me.

She was upstairs trying to find something suitable to put on for the funeral.

I have nothing in black! Nothing that doesn't make me look like a scarecrow.

There was a knock on the door.

My mother said, Answer it. Answer it!

I opened the door and a man was standing there.

If Yuri Gagarin went up into space like some latter day god, Michael O'Shaughnessy seemed to come down out of it.

Descended, not quite like the angel Gabriel it is true, but came there among us like a visitation.

My mother is busy now, I said. Can you come back later?

Quite the little lady, eh? The man said. Tell your Mammy I'll come back tomorrow. There's grief in this house, I've been told, so I'll thank you kindly to pass on my condolences.

Then he gave me a letter which said on the front in neat copper-plate writing, Mrs Esmé Hamilton, The Old Rectory.

Up in the top right hand corner the instruction in capitals BY HAND was appended.

By the time I looked up from the letter, the man had gone again.

What remained was a shadow at the back of my eye, like when you have been looking at the sun too long and the whole world comes back to you in a strange kind of negative.

Ah Michael, that first time I saw you is as fresh now as it ever was. Though the years have passed, and all that is associated with you has been turned to dust.

Rose had written, soliciting a kindness for her sister's son Michael.

Rose is the one who keeps that old place going, was what my grandmother had said very often, with her fingertips resting on a black and white snap of the house she had left so many years previously.

A devout man, is he, your lodger? Mrs Broadbent from the shop asked Momma, measuring out a pound of sausages onto greaseproof paper and folding the ends in.

Handsome in a way, if you like that look, all teeth and eyebrows.

He comes with the highest recommendation.

It was all right in that case, if you knew where a person was from in those days that was all you needed.

Michael is not afraid of hard work and can turn his hand to almost anything.

I went downstairs and into the garden where Michael was bringing it back from wilderness.

He was cutting through the gobbets of red clay soil with an even movement.

With all the respect that is due to you and yours I send my best wishes and hopes that we may meet again in this world or another.

Will you tell me about Ireland, Michael? I said to him.

Ireland? There's nothing much to tell about Ireland, he said.

The house that we lived in was out in the country, at the edge of a village in the middle of nowhere. My grandmother had bought it when she left Ireland after the war that would end all wars and before the start of what became the next one.

She had come back there to that strange border territory, where you look to the west and see legend rising, while behind you in the east the well tended fields of grain and prosperity stretch back to London, that old seat of empire, where fortune is waiting to hand out her spoils to those who are deserving.

My mother had all the old Irish songs, though she had not been back there since she was an infant.

It was too long ago and too far away and the beloved shores were eternally distant.

My Bonnie Maid a' Brownlow go. The Flag of Enniskillen. The Rising of the Moon.

She sang those old songs in a haunting soprano that was filled with low notes.

Your Mammy has a very fine voice, Michael said.

He accompanied her sometimes on a little wooden whistle that he kept in his pocket and had fashioned himself in some foreign clime that still lingered in the wood when you put your hand on it.

He hadn't got the carving quite right, the F-hole I think it was, so no matter what you did, the note came out on the sharp or flat side.

He brings back the life that we lost, Momma said.

He brings back Ireland right up close to me.

And was it not a good thing that Michael O'Shaughnessy was there in the house, a man to attend to things?

Was it not a good thing that he was there as company on the long evenings as dark came down on us?

Was it not a good thing he was there to take me out of myself in this time of bereavement?

A young kind of uncle, in a way, for it was all family over there in Ireland, that is what Granny had used to say, we are all in it together, no matter what class or affiliation.

Hold on tight! Michael said, as he leaned his motorbike hard on the corners and I put my arms around him.

The fields went by shoulder high and the buds on the hedgerows were breaking out into something indefinable.

There was grit in my sandals and my hair was tangled.

His hand was warm as he helped me down again.

Nothing like a ride to shake all the megrims out of you, he said.

Michael O'Shaughnessy had thick black hair that came onto his ears and eyes that took on the flicker of the flames as we sat by the fireside, listening to God Save the Queen on the Third Programme, and hearing how the wind was massing itself at the walls and windows, on the top of that hill, on the edge, whoever heard of building a house in a place like that, much less living in it?

Shall I draw the curtains?

Leave them open, surely.

For the moon was rising and great brittle clouds were fashioning past it.

Time for bed, is it?

It is getting late now.

It has been late always.

I opened *Tropic of Capricorn* and read the following:

Death is behind me and birth too. I am going to live now among the life of maladies.

I wrote in my notebook as the wind was rising, *The house that I live in is at the end of the world.*

On a table in the drawing room was a picture of the *Queen Elizabeth*. We had come back in it from America after my father died.

A fine-looking ship, the *Queen Elizabeth*, Michael said knowledgeably.

I don't remember anything about the voyage except the dislike it gave me for enclosed spaces. And a feeling, perhaps, of extent and motion. Of the horizon always taking itself off from you, and the land of promise, never quite got to, beyond.

Momma had fallen a little in love with a ship's officer.

How could it be otherwise? She was young. She was a widow.

With me trailing behind her, she must have looked enticingly forlorn, in one of those dresses that you wouldn't be seen dead in when you got back to England, ruched at the chest and pinched in at the waistband, so brash, so American, so – *inappropriate*.

She had left with her new and disapproved of husband before the war ended.

If only I'd been here! She would exclaim often, sniffing into a handkerchief that was much too sturdy for the version of the English gentlewoman she was always attempting.

I ran out and left them, she would say on her bad days.

I'm worse than a traitor.

The truth of it was, that my grandmother prospered.

My mother had gone, but she still had Constance.

If you see the old photograph of them together, Esmé and Constance, they do not look remotely like sisters.

Esmé, the copper haired, dark skinned Spaniard, some kind of throw back.

Constance, who narrowly escaped through some mischance the God-given opportunity of being fair and ethereal.

Was my mother jealous of all that she had missed?

The good war?

Was that it?

Even in Kodak's best black and white you can see fire in my mother and my aunt's solidity.

And the past and all that it contained and implied rising up through them like tidal water.

Are they fact or fiction?

The fact is, they are dead now.

And the life they bequeathed me may be no more than a Romance.

My mother met my father on the first day of the blitzkrieg. She had just come out of her last singing lesson when a ripe ten pounder dropped from the sky and demolished a house immediately in front of her.

How strange to see the stairs all naked and the wallpaper hanging. How odd to see a bedstead with its feet over the abyss.

She had been practicing an aria from *Turandot* and her teacher had complimented her on a fine vibrato.

You will go far, Miss O'Donnell, very far indeed with the right coaching.

She could have sung anything. Handel. Verdi.

The world was her oyster.

But the bomb had dropped and there was the man who would become my father not two feet away in his G.I. uniform.

His hat blew off in the blast and he stood there bare headed.

I knew as soon as I saw him, she said. For all that he was shorter than I was, and had an odd way of twisting his shoulder.

The door of the house had swung to and fro as they turned away, but no one came out of it.

Was it love that waylaid her, or some more nefarious interloper?

The heart that beat inside her chest was not meant to beat there in isolation.

That door, swinging to and fro on its hinges.

It was that, more than anything, my mother said afterwards, that sealed her fate.

Nat King Cole sang out on the wireless and my mother sang along with him.

Wenn I faal in lurve

It will be com-pleet-lee

I joined them sometimes in a clear, high voice that echoed right to the top of the house, past the room in the attic where Michael was now, up to the roof where the bats made their signals in the raftered darkness, and emerged with blind certitude into the velvet night.

Or-rile never faal in lurve

Not the Third Programme now, but the Light Programme, that rich honey voice melting the airwaves.

In a rest-less world like this is

Lurve is end-ed bee-fore it's bee-guun

What woman is this who stands before me?

The everyday mother who is ageing and fading, and something beyond that, a symbol, touched if not with divinity then with aspects of the divine.

Too maa-ny moonlight kiss-es
Seem to cool in the warmth of the suun

Will you sing it again, Esmé, Michael says to her.

I pick out the tune on the piano and sing along with Michael in a duet.

Come up, she says. It is getting late now.

I close the lid of the piano and follow her.

Dear God, I intone, kneeling with my bare knees on my bedroom floor while she watches from the doorway. Bring into my life something really important. Grant me, O God, in your divine mercy, the gift of True Love.

My mother tucks in the sheet a little too tightly and bends and kisses me.

That kiss is long gone, sloughed off with a skin so small and tight that it was even then impossible for me to accommodate it.

Lights out.

The house at the end of the world is sleeping.

But the moon shines a way up the twisting stairs that I mount on the tips of my toes like a ballet dancer.

Michael?

I'm here sure enough.

The rustle of bats wings, then his breathing.

Then lowering myself, narrow and naked, into his arms.

Critical Triumph for a Long Banned Book!

The type-face was artlessly simple and in tune with itself, pronouncing an age that has entirely gone from us, when you took yourself and everyone else more or less seriously, and sex was a bit like eating lemon sherbet in the playground, you contemplated your discoloured finger for a long time afterwards, and remembered the taste and scent of it ages after the guilt and the pleasure had faded, and the way the decadence sizzled on the surface of your tongue.

A grand paean to all that is still joyous, healthy, happy and affirmative in this age of atomic bombs.

The exclamation mark was missing, but it was very much implied.

Michael, I said, what does paean mean?

There was no answer.

Michael, are you listening?

But he wasn't listening, he was watching his hand and the circle of it compassed by my ribs where the skin went down tight and shiny over my diaphragm, and that little bony hillock to the south, as yet almost unforested, that the heel of his thumb bumped up against sometimes and sent a tremor out through my hip joints and down into the tender greenwood of the bones of my thighs.

Miller has once and for all blasted the very foundations of human hypocrisy – moral, social and political.

I looked at the front of Michael O'Shaughnessy's pyjamas and I knew what was coming.

Will you get on top of me, Michael said.

It was a very good thing I had read Henry Miller because I knew what to do when Michael asked me.

Or I knew what I thought I should do, and what he did himself came as no surprise to me.

I understood, which I wouldn't have done otherwise, when Michael seemed to be getting beside himself. I had never seen anybody beside themselves in that way in my life. His eyes shut and his face screwed up and he jerked about as though he was having a fit. But that was alright because it was what Henry described as transports. It was pleasure, not pain, I was clear on that much.

He held me very tightly as I lowered myself on the way he had taught me.

It felt interesting, that was all. I knew from reading Henry that something else was supposed to happen. I had been particularly struck by the passage about the Jewish girl, the one that goes, *Suddenly I could feel her begin coming, a long drawn out orgasm such as you sometimes get with Jewish cunts.*

I didn't know what the words meant but I knew from the description you were supposed to moan and shudder. I had been pretty silent in the times up to now when I had straddled Michael, content to watch him rock backwards and forwards, until, after an interval which got a bit boring, he'd sit half upright and hold still for an instant, and jerk his head back, and shout.

Shift up a bit.

Now down.

It seemed to take a long time for his face to start to get contorted. The bedspring squeaked and I counted to a hundred. I thought perhaps I should do something, so I began to moan.

Michael said,

Hush.

The concentrated look had just about come to him when I started to get uncomfortable through being so long in the one position. The way he was holding me kept all the weight of my body on the fronts of my knees.

Keep still, Michael said.

Almost immediately after, something hurt for a second, and I jumped and said,

Ow.

Michael groaned and said,

Come off me now, quickly.

I lay on my back, grateful to be able to stretch out my legs, and he set about things from on top of me.

The bedsprings were squeaking, frantically, frantically.

I heard a bat up above me in the rafters on its nightly journey.

I saw in my mind's eye it's stretched out wings transparent on the roof struts.

Squeak-squeak-squeak-squeak-squeak-squeak-squeak-squeak.

Michael, I said after a minute, very politely. Excuse me. You're lying on my hair.

Christ! Michael O'Shaughnessy said.

I was brought up in that peculiar twilight zone that is life under threat of annihilation.

The war was over, but a yellowing ration book with a few pages left in it came to the surface sometimes in the kitchen drawer.

Hiroshima was a name engraved on the age, and next to it, in smaller letters, Nagasaki.

I looked up at aeroplanes crossing the sky and shaded my eyes so that I could see their markings.

I imagined how the moment of attack would be, and threw myself down in the grass and covered my head with my arms in the way I knew you were supposed to.

I picked up a thin-looking leaflet at the dentist's, with diagrams in it, that said, *What to Do in the Event of a Nuclear Attack.*

The Winds of Change were blowing through Africa, though they didn't seem to reach us there on the top of that hill where we lived as though on an island, marooned or shipwrecked.

I've been to the doctor, Momma said, and he's given me something. Let's hope it works this time.

Harold MacMillan had assured us that a new age was dawning. Austerity was ending. We had never had it so good.

Parcels came sometimes with a New York stamp on them.

Brown paper parcels tied up with string and sealed with a red blob of sealing wax where the string crossed over.

Imagine the Polanskis remembering us still!

Remembering their old neighbours all this time later.

Tins of ripe peaches in a golden syrup.

Cans of Fray Bentos with a key on the side that you wound to open them.

How kind it was, how thoughtful and considerate.

Just a little something to help out in these difficult times, the appended note said.

And a chocolate bar and a ten dollar bill for the little Babushka.

They were thinking of us still. How that warmed the heart!

But I heard my mother saying later to my grandmother, That's the fucking Yanks all over. Don't they just like to grind our noses in it. Come in at the last minute and think they've won the war.

If any man ever dared to translate all that is in his heart the world would go to smash, and no god, no accident, no will could ever again assemble the pieces.

I used to believe that each person is responsible for whatever has befallen them, that the living and breathing self that has taken this choice or that choice and left the others in the gutter of existence is what determines things.

But lately I have come to understand that we are subject to forces, or at least to the culmination of events that occur in the wider scheme of things that we have no control over.

The official Soviet news agency Tass has announced that a Russian astronaut, Major Yuri Gagarin, is the first man in space.

The end of the horizon as my grandmother knew it.

Imagination could no longer be what it was, the perspectives were different.

And the Annie that I was?

If you reel time back then nothing at all would be as it has been.

No Henry Miller, no fucking and carousing, no war, no British Empire, no America.

No Momma. No Daddy with his hands clutched to his chest in a rictus.

No capsule up there with the human frame impaled on the instant of man's greatest achievement.

I am crying for more and more disasters, for bigger calamities, grander failures.

Make the wind blow more strongly, O God, I prayed, make the gale attend, make the waves lash up, make night more dark and day more dazzling, make eternity more eternal than it is, but please do something!

I looked at the face of the saviour with the halo suspended, and transposed the visage of Henry Miller onto those features with the light behind them.

Do anything, but let it produce joy. Do anything, but let it yield ecstasy!

Was it love that I wanted?

Or was what I wanted action, action, to be doing, not done to, in a world that was spinning towards its own conflagration at every sunset?

I lay in my bed with the moon coming in through the undrawn curtain.

I heard Michael's voice and his step on the stair and what I was and what he was and what the world in all its splendour *could* be were all amalgamated there in the vortex of dream that I went down into.

I heard the door click, and Michael's motorbike revving up through the remains of the night that hung like a web still, just above the driveway.

Where there was silence, I would make sound occur, where there was stillness, I would make movement.

Inner and outer have changed places. Equilibrium is no longer the goal — the scales must be destroyed.

I got up and went to the window and watched as Michael rode away through the gates that were always open and along the lane to where the walls took over and the hedges obliterated him.

I turned back into the room that was mine, and the house, and the life, and I heard the first sounds quite a long way off of my mother stirring.

Oh Henry, make me other than I am, I said. Make me something remarkable.

My mother called Annie, Annie! and I knew from her voice it was one of her bad days.

Henry had not answered immediately, but he would do.

He was out there waiting. I was hand in glove with my fate.

My grandmother had a lock of her husband's hair with *her* mother's, in a mourning brooch.

It makes them seem nearer, somehow, Momma said, cradling the brooch in the palm of her hand as though it was liquid.

Two little cuttings of hair, very dry-looking, nestled together behind the glass. That oval glass, no more than an inch and a bit wide, gave to my living a peculiar urgency.

Granny had begun to decline at the end of the winter.

The days were just beginning to lengthen.

She had been out planting seeds and when she came in again she said, I don't feel too well now.

The next day a pinched look came to her.

I heard Momma speaking on the telephone later.

The doctor has told me it's only a matter of time.

I watched the grandfather clock in the hall with a new attention. It's amazing, the resonance attention will give to a tick. It had a particular timbre. As though it was half of a dialogue, and you the missing half, because you didn't understand the language.

At times I thought I was on the point of understanding, but I never really did understand. It was more important for me not to understand. It gave me the courage to stand alone, it enabled me to appreciate loneliness.

Not long after Granny got her pinched look, I took to practicing the piano daily.

Don't disturb your grandmother with a row.

There wasn't much danger of that because her bedroom, which she very soon took to, was right on the other side of the house.

It wasn't a very exciting piano, just a rosewood upright, rather out of tune, with filled-up bits in the front of it where they had taken the candelabra out.

They used to have such accidents in the old days, Granny had said to me.

When you leaned forward your sleeve or your hair would get caught in the candle flame.

I wondered what it would be like to ignite on the final phrase of some stumbled piece, *Greensleeves*, or *Where E're You Walk*. Go up, you know, like a torch, with a *whoosh* and a crackle.

I set out the metronome and played in time to it.

I would set it very fast and tumble through the exercises.

I would set it painfully slow, so that an age elapsed almost between one note and the next.

From the beginning it was never anything but chaos; it was a fluid which enveloped me, which I breathed in through the gills.

Oh Henry Miller, what language did you teach me?

A language which I came to as naturally as to the dream of the land beyond the boundary.

There was a record in the cupboard which I took out sometimes and played on the gramophone, lowering the needle down carefully to the groove which picked up the scratchy rendition of Madame Butterfly's great aria, *One Day My Love Will Come*.

There was a white label on it, somewhat discoloured, which said in black handwriting, *Esmé Recording 1948. Quantas Studios. Nth 42nd Street.*

Will you sing it to me Momma?

Not now.

Not ever.

For the red satin dress with the low cut bodice has been hung up in the wardrobe for many a year now.

The long chiffon wrap with the tarnished sequins is hanging next to it.

Emblems.

Reminders.

A fine vibrato.

She could have done so much with it.

For God's sake will you put that away, she says to me.

It's history. The whole fucking lot is history and has been for a long time.

The metronome set.

Ticktickticktickticktickticktick.

It was as though my mother fed me a poison. I was corrupt from the start.

My grandmother stipulated that she was to be cremated. Her ashes were to be scattered at the crematorium. No stone or monument was to be erected. Nothing visible or lasting was to be set up to remember her by.

I've always thought I would like to preserve my bloodless, gutless body for as long as possible in a lead coffin, preferably in a crypt, on a stone shelf with a big stone lid on it, the sort of place you go down steps to get to, and carved very deeply above me, my birth and death dates, and after them, my full name.

I have waded through the river of death many times but the light that's in me refuses to be extinguished.

Ah Henry, that is what I gleaned from you, in those early days of our acquaintance.

What I want is to open up – to open up the earth. I know that underneath the mess everything is marvellous.

What's that you're reading?

Nothing. Nothing.

I think a nice cross on the order of service, the undertaker says. You can't go wrong with a nice cross, can you?

Is it only those of us who are corrupt who want to be immortal?

Ticktickticktickticktickticktick.

Stop that now, Momma says to me.

Obediently I shut the lid and put away the music.

Come up and see your grandmother. Seeing you will cheer her. She's feeling a little low.

I go up the stairs very slowly, with my feet feeling heavy. Outside the bedroom, with the door ajar, I pause. The smell of death comes to me, and antiseptic.

Slowly, I push back the door.

Babushka, the little voice says.

The hand, with its fingers, lifts uncertainly on the sheet.

I sit in the stillness with the light moving through the room.

Perhaps you could read to me, Granny says. Such a reader, my granddaughter. Such a little thinker, already.

That was what I had in common with Henry. All there was to pit against chaos were words, and a little off-key music, and the sweet epiphany of the metronome.

We were going to Ireland, all three of us.

That was the plan.

There had never been a plan as good as this one.

Michael would go ahead of us on his bike, and Momma and I would follow by car, taking the ferry from Fishguard to Rosslare, a great adventure, and then we would drive through the fine country-side that led up to the old house, and Rose would be there as she always had been, and there would be something in the way of a rec-onciliation, the past and the present brought together again, Ireland reconstituted, a warm reunion.

We'll take Granny with us, do you see? Momma said. We'll take her back to where she came from.

For the ashes had not yet been scattered at the crematorium as Granny had instructed.

If she had thought that going back to the old house was possible, she would surely have wished it, was Momma's rationale for the pro-posed change of resting place for Granny's remains, which were in a white urn in the kitchen cabinet, next to the jars which said 'Flour' and 'Sugar' and 'Suet for dumplings'.

It was all arranged and the tickets were bought but when Momma woke up on the morning of departure she said, I can't do this.

She had a new supply of pills from the doctor that she put a lot of faith in.

She had brought them home in a white cardboard box which said on the side, For Grief. Take two as recommended.

The doctor says these are stronger and will help me. I don't know what I'll do if they don't.

On the morning we were due to leave she woke up and was crying a lot.

What am I going to do in this world? She said, stroking the urn that had Granny in it.

What am I going to do here alone?

When Michael came in and said it was time we were leaving she said, I'm not going. I'm not up to it. Annie will take care of the urn and go with you.

She turned to me then.

You're up to it, aren't you, Annie? Granny would have liked that. Her little Babushka finally putting her to rest.

The crossing was a rough one.

Granny's ashes had been transferred to a smaller container that had been a tea caddy, entirely appropriate in Momma's view since Granny's husband had once been in tea with the East India company.

Michael sealed up the tin with brown parcel tape and said, That'll keep her safe for the journey.

She nestled at the bottom of my knapsack out of harm's way and impervious to sea air and accidents.

It was only a four hour crossing so Michael hadn't got us a cabin.

We found a place to sit up against a window and Michael settled with his feet up somewhere they shouldn't have been and said, It's going to be a rough night.

I knew what he meant as soon as we got out of the harbour. There was a wind such as you wouldn't really have expected.

The boat started rolling and yawing. It was pitch black, and every so often the sea crashed up against the window, leaving behind it a pattern of white foam.

Michael, I said.

Go to sleep, he said. Wedge your head up against my shoulder.

I lay with my forehead tucked up to his chest and listened to his breathing.

Why does your heart beat like that? I said.

Like what? he said.

Like it's going off in a kind of explosion.

He laughed and said,

If I were you, I wouldn't worry about it.

As we got to Rosslare it was a lot calmer. The dawn was grey and watery.

Michael said,

Wait there.

He came back smelling of bacon and carrying a hot sandwich.

Eat that, he said. It'll make you feel better.

The land was much closer and you could see the detail of it. Michael looked at his watch and said,

You've got grease on your cheek and your mouth needs wiping.

He took me below and found a cabin that had been vacated.

He used one of the towels that had been thrown down by the basin to wipe my face with.

That's better, he said. Now, brush your teeth with your finger.

I did as he told me and, trying to make a good job of it, combed out my hair.

He looked me over and said,

You look like a bit of a Gyppo. Come here.

He'd locked the door of the cabin so I had an idea what was going to happen.

He kissed me with the inside of his lips all open and I responded, the way he'd taught me, with my tongue.

I thought he'd want to lie down, but he didn't. Her lifted my leg up quite high and set himself into me standing. Then he used just the end of it, gently, with his hands holding me apart. A warm feeling started to come over me. I knew he was watching my expression but I didn't care. I said,

Michael.

I couldn't do anything about it. My eyes closed.

When I opened them again he was grinning a bit which I didn't like because it made him look half-baked.

Did you like that? he said.

I said,

Partly.

I wasn't going to have him thinking too much of himself.

Which part did you like best?

When you let me go, I said.

I grew up quite a lot, riding round Ireland with Michael.

I rode up behind him with my arms tight round his waist, and screamed when he leaned the bike over too far on the corners.

We roared around the countryside, out in the middle of nowhere, and he took me with him in the evenings into pubs which had sawdust on the floor and spittoons, and a privy, if you were lucky, with an Elsan in it, and a ragged bit of some old towel to wipe your hands.

There were young men and old men that Michael talked to.

Through the pipe smoke I would watch him talk and gesticulate.

He looked young to me then, younger than he had a right to.

Are you all right there with your book, now, Annie? It's a great crack this. There's nothing like it.

Sometimes we stayed in a Bed and Breakfast, where he would pretend to be my father. When he pretended to be that he acted like it too, so we were both glad to get out. Mostly we camped, right out in the wilds.

None of it was very hygienic. The groundsheet leaked and we slept perpetually damp. Michael made a fire one night, and we took all our clothes off and dried them. While they were drying he lay out on the ground on a blanket and said,

Will you get on top of me.

We did it like that, right out in the open, both of us naked, and I could see he wanted the same thing to happen that had in the cabin, so I said,

Michael, trying to make it the same voice.

He said,

For God's sake stop pretending.

It came to me suddenly that something was wrong with it.

I got right up off him, just like that, and ran off naked across the field.

He took a moment to collect himself, then he ran after me, and he looked very funny, holding himself and stumbling when he stepped on a thistle, and yelling.

He caught me up when I'd stopped because of the river. It was well into dusk, so I didn't at all want to swim it. The water looked solid, almost, with a skin on it.

You're a fucking maniac, Annie, that's what you are, Michael said.

He was shivering a bit and his flesh looked white in the twilight.

And next time, will you fucking well come when I call you, he said.

That was the moment when I lost my innocence.

My feet are covered in sheep shit, I said.

The sea was a blue sheet and the world was smiling and sunny.

We were way up above it, just like the film they made in Kerry.

He'd been using his tongue and his lips, just sucking, as though it were a dummy.

If only men knew, they don't have to do anything fancy. Just keep it up, whatever it is you've found out she likes, in a rhythm.

Of all things I've always abhorred, it's a man who's in a hurry.

Michael had the timing of it perfectly. It felt as though he wouldn't have minded spending all day.

I think what's essential is knowing they can make you do it. Knowing they're willing to put up with your fright and uncertainties.

I don't believe that any of Henry Miller's women came.

I bet they were all just pretending.

The thing is, I don't just do it once like other women. I keep on doing it. If you keep on doing it, like that, you've really got to trust a man.

I heard myself doing and doing it. I sounded as though I was in pain.

Michael didn't tell me to stop pretending.

Instead he said Darling, and Darling again.

We scrambled down to the beach and wandered there after. It was quite romantic, with Michael holding my hand.

I felt as though I was a thousand years old.

Michael put his arm round my shoulders, expansive. We'd been talking about this and that, and the future.

What d'you want to be when you grow up, Annie, he asked me.

I felt like I'd felt when his lips had been drawing myself out of me.

My language, my world, is under my arm. I am the guardian of a great secret.

I didn't answer, for a minute.

The sea had got still and the mountains, so beautiful, had turned into iron beside it.

Far out, a gull dived full tilt into the water. From the splash it arose as a shadow.

No sorrows, no regrets, no past, no future.

I'm going to be a writer, I said.

It rained on the way to Dublin. Michael said he had to visit his family there.

On the bridge with the water very brown underneath it there were people begging.

Tinkers, Michael said.

It was a grand sort of city but had a sad feel that I couldn't put my finger on.

We crossed the bridge into a very wide street and Michael said, This is O'Connell Street.

About half way up was a statue of Horatio Nelson.

He looked like he was pronouncing somehow, or laying down a law.

Michael told me it was only by the grace of God that the thing was still standing, for a few years before that, some students had tried to burn it down with a flamethrower

I asked him why they did that and he said,

Why shouldn't they?

We stood at the bottom and looked up at the great man and Michael said, He'll be gone from here one day.

Then he took me down to the far end of the street and said, This here's Parnell. He was a real Irishman, and no mistaking.

Parnell was looking out from his plinth with what seemed to me a benign expression.

See those marks there? Michael said. That's where the bullets hit the stonework in the Easter Rising. There's a lot of history in this city, that's for sure.

The black of the traffic was everywhere.

It's a hell-hole, Dublin, Michael said, but I love it.

His family lived in a run-down house in a street called York Street.

God, I said, were you brought up here?

I was, he said.

But it turned out after that he was not.

York Street was narrower than the others and had papers blowing about and was criss-crossed by potholes.

When Michael knocked on the door of Number 47 there was no sound inside and he knocked again and a voice said, Will you wait, why can't you? And then we heard footsteps coming slowly down the stairs.

Mother, he introduced me. This is Annie.

She was a small woman with a neat apron going up over her shoulders.

How do, she said. Then she said, it's a long time since we've seen you, Michael.

It is that, Michael said. But I'm here now anyway.

He had two sisters who were out working in the factory. He was the apple of his mother's eye, you could tell that much.

His father was down at the shipyard, on the evening shift.

We'll miss him then, Michael said. That's a pity.

You'll surely be staying? his mother asked him.

No, Ma. I'm sorry. We've got to get on, he said.

The bedroom they put me to stay in was with one of the sisters. Her name was Katy but for some reason I couldn't fathom they called her Maire. She had eyes like Michael.

The other was Eliza, and her face was wizzened and her head was sharp as a pin.

She asked me how I liked riding round the country with Michael.

Oh, I like it, I said.

It was all very above board and proper.

You know that Jo is in England now, Michael? The one that was Maire said. But we don't hear much from him.

There was an older brother, whose name I did not catch, who was up in the country again, trying his hand at the farming, but nobody knew what good would come of it.

I didn't know you had such a family, I said to Michael.

Eliza looked at me hard and said,

Our Michael was always a close one.

Michael said,

That's enough now.

That's families for you, the mother said, twisting the dish rag up in her hands like it was a lifeline.

You do what you can for them. You never know where it will end.

They put me to sleep in the room on what they called a truckle. There was a jug and a basin on the washstand, and a folded up towel.

The sister called Maire lent me a winceyette nightdress. It had sprigs of blue flower on it, lavender or bluebell.

Eliza was to go to a neighbour so Michael could have her bed.

Maire brought in a pan of hot water and gave it to me.

That's special treatment, Eliza said. I'd like hot water.

I washed with them watching. As I reached under my nightgown I thought of Michael.

Good night, now, Annie, he said, and did not kiss me.

I took out Miller and consulted him under the sheet.

Was it a cold light that greeted us the following morning, or was it neutral?

It has seemed to me often that the world lets you know in advance what will be the shape of things.

Your own little fate, no matter how small it may be, is etched in the pattern of events and happenings.

The life that was Annie's was there in the light and the air of that Dublin morning.

It was there in the scent and the taste of it all, in the grain of the day as it formed around us.

I packed up my kitbag with the sisters watching me.

Michael had said we should leave early. We had miles to go before we got to the old place, and the roads up to it were not direct ones.

You've got fine things there, Eliza said, watching me repack the tin that had Granny in it, then put in Miller.

What's the first line of the book? Can you tell us that? It has the look of a fine book, that one.

Once you have given up the ghost, I recited, *everything follows with dead certainty.*

Well, that's not much of a way to start a story, now is it, Eliza said.

The father was back and sitting with Michael and the mother in the next room.

He had come in from the shipyard and had hollows under his eyes.

So this is the little girl, is it? He said.

She doesn't look so little to me, but then, you are the judge of it.

They'll be moving us out of here soon, the mother was saying. It's the Corporation. It might be the Griffith Barracks, but I hope it won't be.

Michael tells me you're a reader, the father said to me then, and you're all set to be a scholar one day.

When I nodded he said, Trinity College or some such place. That is where Michael tells me you're destined.

I told him I'd be going to Oxford most probably, and he pursed his lips and said something under his breath.

Eliza came in then with Granny in her left hand and Henry Miller held in her right.

What's this, she said. Tea? We could do with some tea.

It's my grandmother's ashes.

Holy Mother of God!

She dropped both the book and the tin, and the tin stayed intact but the book fell open.

What's this now, the father said, picking it up.

Annie's for reading and reading, Michael said.

He looked the nearest I'd seen him to being uncomfortable.

What's a young girl reading these days, I'd like to know, the father said.

He handed the book to Eliza and said, Read something out. My eyes are tired now.

The mother said, Eliza's a very good reader. Has won prizes. I was a great reader once, but it soon came to be that I didn't have the time for it.

Eliza began reading in a sing song voice, as she had clearly learned to recite the catechism.

You can forgive a young cunt anything. A young cunt doesn't have to have brains. They're better without brains. But an old cunt, even if she's brilliant, nothing makes any difference. A young cunt is an investment; an old cunt is a dead loss.

There was a silence in which you could hear a pin drop.

That's Henry Miller, I said, as if I was trying to be helpful. It's called *Tropic of Capricorn*, in case you'd like to know the title.

Miller? Miller?

The father was bellowing.

What is this filth? What is this iniquity?

He looked like a bull. His eyes were bloodshot.

Now, father, the poor mother said, bowing her shoulders.

No girl that's reading such stuff should have spent the night under my roof.

We're catching the four o'clock ferry, Michael said.

Shame on you, Michael, the father said, to bring such a trollop and a doxy among us. It was always the same. It was always like you.

Now, Pat, she's a child still – , the mother began.

Child or not, take a look at the eyes on her! She's a hussy, more like it. Have a care, I'd say, for your son.

What did you go and do that for? Michael asked me.

We'd packed in a hurry and left instanter.

I didn't tell him the truth, which was that I hated his family.

I didn't do anything, I said. It was Eliza.

Yes you did, and you did it on purpose.

We were sitting on a bench in the city and the fumes from the traffic were getting into my lungs.

I coughed in my hand and hoped Michael would notice.

Stop that, he said. I'm damned if I'm going to baby you.

There was a coolness developed between us.

I ate bacon listlessly in a seedy cafe.

We walked on the docks and watched the cranes working. It made me dizzy, tilting my head back and looking up so high.

You shouldn't have upset the old man, Michael said.

I hated the house, and them, and everything in it.

He put his hands in his pockets and walked on a step ahead of me, whistling.

Not good enough for you, he said.

No, I said.

We stopped on a windswept corner while Michael got the map out.

The sea was behind us, a smudge of blue smoke that the wind might blow away.

Ahead of us were mountains, rather black looking and inhospitable.

It's up here now ahead of us for sure, Michael said.

We set off again as the clouds came in over us, a thin mist and a chill one, and I zipped my jacket up.

The low walls flashed past us in their stony desuetude.

We skirted a pine wood then went over the top of a range that had the cloud down.

I felt fear for a moment that Michael would lose the steep road and come off at a corner and plunge – who knew where? To the lough I saw glittering at the foot of the range, its surface encrypted in ripples like the tucks of a little girl's dress all laid out for a party.

We were right down out of it.

Michael shouted something which I did not hear for the wind whipped it past me.

Then, up a long narrow lane which turned and twisted.

Sometimes you went forward and sometimes you seemed only to be coming back on yourself.

The dusk was thickening in the hedges around us and I heard how a lone bird sang its farewell to the day in a Scots pine that stood by the bend where the bike turned off as if of its own will, nosing through fern and dark rhododendron, around puddles and potholes and bits of white picket fence with gates that led nowhere but into the undergrowth.

We came out in a space and the house stood before us.

In the silence that followed Michael switching off the engine I leaped down and ran at full tilt towards it.

The last rays of the sun lit the lake and the side of the house was an orange firewall.

The sky flipped around and I lay there winded.

That nasty old wire in the grass has tripped you.

The woman I saw standing above me gave her hand to Michael.

It's been a long time.

It has been, but I'm here now.

As I got to my feet the world righted and Michael said, Annie. This is Rose.

We did not distribute Granny's ashes immediately. The thing was to be done with due pomp and ceremony, Rose would have it.

She got Father Leavy to come up from the village.

He had not known my grandmother, he said, but his predecessor had known all of my relatives.

There was a plaque in the church in memory of my grandfather Theodore that I might like to look at some day.

Meanwhile it was our bounden duty to see the ashes of my grandmother to their final rest.

She wasn't a Catholic, I said to Michael.

That doesn't matter. Father Leavy is a good one.

And indeed on that day in its wholesale benignity we all seemed good.

As the Father spoke words which rose up in their beauty far higher than Yuri Gagarin could aspire to, the wind took the flakes of what had been flesh, and lifted and dropped them in a random pattern.

When it was over, Rose went with the Father and Michael went fishing.

You'd better be careful what you catch out there, Michael, the Father said.

The disorientation and reorientation which comes with the initiation into any mystery is the most wonderful experience.

I see you've found it.

Father Leavy is standing in the doorway.

The sun has gone down lower in the sky. I am in the room that they call the library. It is a locked up room and I think I'm not supposed to be there. It smells musty, and bears the jaw-marks of silver fish.

Rose sent me back, he is saying now. She thought you might come here.

Is it wrong to come?

I hear you're a book lover, the father says.

He picks up the album I've been perusing.

Clanpellan Hall, 1925, a musical interlude, he reads out loud. That's a fine photo. But your grandmother was a fine women, so I'm led to believe. God rest her easy.

There is the image enmeshed in my brain.

A pale afternoon of tea and ices.

Straight little dresses and cloche hats and neat little shoes with bows at the instep and a string quartet playing in the shade of a lime tree.

My grandmother, unmistakable as the life that was hers until recently.

Turning her two little girls in the direction of the camera.

Constance and Esmé.

Wrinkling her eyes up and putting her hand to her forehead to stave off the low rays of sun that are coming in flatly from the west already.

The house is behind them.

Nothing has changed.

Time does not exist here.

It's all right to grieve. We all have to grieve, the Father says, his hand on my shoulder.

I take the book from him and close it up and put it back down in its place precisely.

Is it all right with Michael? the Father says then. Does he treat you properly?

Oh he does, I say. He does treat me properly.

You'd tell me if anything was troubling you, would you?

A sound outside. A human sound, is it? A man going by with a shuffling step, pushing a barrow and with a rake on his shoulder. His mouth moving and random things that are not quite words coming out of it.

The mad bring good luck, so they say, but I doubt that, the Father says.

Poor Shane Paul is a help to Rose, he says, raising his hand and letting it fall again.

She needs all the help she can get with this place.

Does no one else come now?

They have not for a long time.

A shame and a pity, that is for certain, but you take what is dished out to you in this life of grace.

Rose was sorry to see us go.

Michael had told her that my Mammy was a little soft in the head these days, and it was best if we got back there.

She hoped, she said to me, that Michael was giving satisfaction?

It was a responsibility, to give such a recommendation as she had.

She gave me a little white prayer book and a rosary.

A refuge and a solace in time of trouble.

I thanked her and put them next to Miller in my knapsack.

It was good, she said, to see I was a reader. If more people were reading, the world would be a better place.

There was no wind at all when we crossed back over. It was so calm, I swear, that you could have got there on a pair of roller skates.

There was a woman opposite Michael who crossed and uncrossed her legs and smiled a lot.

She asked him how old his little daughter was and he gave the wrong age.

She said would my mummy be meeting me and he said no. Then he said he was a widower and that looked as if it impressed her and she said could she get us both some tea.

After the tea I dozed a bit and they went on talking, leaning towards one another over their feet.

It was darkish as we got into Fishguard. There was a light drizzle that was set into your face by the wind. On deck, they handed each other folded up pieces of paper. I didn't ask what they were.

When will you be seeing her again? I said to him. She'd gone down the gangplank and we were standing looking after her.

She turned and Michael waved from the railing.

Sometime. But come on now, he said.

In the house, nothing seemed to be different.

Momma was pleased to see us and, that first day, seemed to be brighter.

The house was a bit of a mess so I set about cleaning it. Then I did some washing because Momma had forgotten all about clean clothes.

In the evening, when Michael had gone out, she roused herself.

Did you enjoy it, *Babushka*? Now, really?

I did, Momma, I did enjoy it, I replied.

I showed her the prayer book and the rosary that Rose had given me.

She held them in her hand for a minute then turned them very carefully to the light.

Things have their moment, she said. You don't know that yet, but one day you will do.

Someone in the village asked me when Michael was leaving, she said then. Did you know anything about a job with a lodging in Newport?

I didn't know anything about any job, I said.

As it happened he did have a job but he stayed lodging with us which was just as well because very soon after we came back Momma went funny.

God, she's gone over the edge this time and no mistaking, Michael said.

She did not get up, for what was the point of it?

What was the point of anything, really?

You'll have to go in, I'm afraid, the Doctor said.

Momma said nothing.

The Doctor shut his big black bag with a click.

You'll have to be very grown-up now Annie, he said as he was leaving.

But you'll be all right, won't you? You'll be at school in the daytime and in the night time there'll be Michael O'Shaughnessy to look after you.

They called it Anxiety Neurosis. What it meant was, Momma sat there all day in a corner, crying and shivering, in a heap.

I think I'm going to kill myself, she said.

How could they go off like that and leave me? Your father. Your grandmother. And even when I was a little thing, little and hardly able to fend for myself, he went off, Daddy, and left me. Oh, what am I going to do in a world like this? What am I going to do here, alone?

The only treatment they had for it, the doctor said, was putting electric shocks through you to burn out the bad bits.

They can't burn this out, Momma said. It's here in my head. It's all that has happened. If they burn that out, they'll burn out the rest of me.

Michael said he would take her in on his motor bike.

You could ride up there pillion, Esmé, he said. We'd make a sight of it.

The doctor wouldn't hear of it however, and arranged to take her himself, in his car.

We must pull together, now mustn't we, Esmé, the doctor said to her. For the sake of the girl. The girl is what matters. It's her future, and you're all she has now, don't you think so?

What I go back to again and again, and did do then, and will do always, is when Momma said it to me and I didn't know what to do and I did nothing, just went down the stairs and left her and walked round the garden with my arms around me, like they are when you're wearing a strait-jacket, the fingers pointing backwards along the sides of your ribs and the elbows crossed in front of you.

I wanted to scream out then, but the voice within me was silent. There is nothing so profound as the silence of inarticulation. The whole weight of the world was in chains on my tongue.

But who in any case could I have told?

Babushka, she said.

When she grasped my arm the hairs stood up around her fingers in a delicate forest.

Babushka. I have a secret to tell you.

She pulled me down beside her on the bed.

Ah!

She lay back on the pillows in a white nightdress with her hair down. There was grey in the dark mass of it, which surprised me.

You know what death is, my baby?

I know it, Momma, I said.

She smiled, as if in satisfaction.

You know what a promise is, too?

I nodded.

I want you to make me a promise.

She paused for a moment.

You know what it means to swear?

To swear means to promise on all you know to be Holy.

That's my *Babushka*. That's my good little girl, she said.

She smiled and suddenly she was as she had been before.

Do you swear never to tell a soul the secret I'm telling you?

I swear, Momma, I said.

All that was strange in her had gone, and I kissed her.

I was her daughter.

She reached for the bottle that was on her bedside table. I remember the slow way she unfolded her arm.

I read what was on the label carefully, because she told me to.

The room was suddenly strange, in its separate pieces.

There was a single pill, black, in the bottom of the bottle.

I've taken the others, she said. I've taken all of them.

The look on her face was beatific.

I'm dying at this very moment. Yes, dying. You'll be better off without me, *Babushka*, she said.

I was on top of Michael, he was having to work very hard at it, he could tell my mind was elsewhere, maybe.

Will you shift that way a bit, he told me, and I did.

Suddenly she let out a wail and he said,

Christ! She sounds like a bloody banshee!

He put me off him and leaned sulky on his elbow and said,

Will you go in there maybe and do something to calm her?

I said,

No.

The bedside light was on and his head cast a long shadow on the wall. It was the shadow, I can remember thinking, of the Neanderthal.

My own shadow was a poor thin thing, like a wisp of something.

She went on wailing and he got a bit frightened and went in to her himself.

When he came out he looked white and said,

Where's the telephone?

I think he must have forgotten.

I said,

Michael. Your flies are open.

He said,

Mary Mother of God and All the Saints.

When the ambulance had come and taken her, he came into my room and took away the book I was reading.

Still this filth, he said.

You should try reading it, I said.

A good Catholic can't read Miller, he retorted.

He moved about the room for a minute and I watched him. He was rubbing the hairs on the back of his neck with his hand. He got hold of me and said,

Now, Annie. Did you know anything about it?

About what? I said.

You know, he said.

No, I said.

You're a bloody little liar when all's said and done, he said, letting go of my shoulder.

She's a mad woman, he said under his breath. Then to me,

You shouldn't have anything to do with it.

He sat on the bed then with his head in his hands and I heard some word come out of him which sounded like 'pity'.

I was snivelling a bit while he did it to me and I think it must have put him off because he said,

Quiet it, will you?

I tried breathing differently but it didn't make much difference because he soon said,

God, it's hopeless, and got me to lie down beside him.

Are you warm enough? he said.

No, I said.

Here, he said, and held me tight against him, and pulled up the quilt.

You could see the moon, hazy with an amber halo around it.

It looks like somebody breathed on the moon, I said.

Shall I go to school? I asked Michael the next day. There's a week to go to the holidays.

Do what you like. But I don't see why you should bother.

He wrote me a sick note in his careful handwriting, but I tore up what he'd done and wrote one myself, I could forge it better.

In the evenings I cooked something for him, as well as I could, and he helped me.

He said that I wasn't to go to him at night in the attic.

It wouldn't be right. It'd be taking advantage, with your mother gone off to the hospital, he said.

I said,

But Michael, don't you want me to get on top of you?

He looked down at the floor and said nothing.

I liked it when you sucked me, I said.

He said,

Annie, forget it. All that's in the past now.

The house was so big and so quiet I was afraid to move. I would sit like a mouse on the sofa hour after hour. If I was feeling brave I would turn on the wireless. It was *Housewives Choice* and *Mrs Dale's Diary* and *Worker's Playtime*. But the sound, by the end of the morning, got on my nerves.

Very often, I was dying to go to the lavatory. When I had to, I would run through the hall with a pack of wolves at my heels. When I had washed my hands, I would wait at the foot of the stairs, afraid to re-cross the long window. I thought that a man with a gun was waiting outside.

Why are you sitting in the dark? Michael would ask me.

Thinking. I was just thinking. And waiting for you to come home, I said.

The bit of Miller that Michael liked best was the scene with the twat and the carrot.

Miller recounts how a friend is fucking a Miss Abercrombie who can't get enough, so he shoves in a carrot for a joke, and she doesn't notice.

Michael always laughed heartily when I read it to him.

A right old biddy *she* must have been, he generally said.

It was Miller who got us into perversions. Not that we did anything very terrible.

Do you think you'd know the difference if it was a carrot? Michael asked me.

I don't know, I said.

Do you think it might be interesting to find out?

I could have quoted page after page of Miller from memory.

I read him from start to finish and when I had finished I started reading him again.

The repetition of it was a comfort, knowing which bits went where.

If this book had not fallen into my hands at the precise moment it did, perhaps I would have gone mad. It came at a moment when a huge world was crumbling.

Michael had soon forgotten all about taking advantage. He came to my bed, because it was bigger, and made very obvious jokes of my books and my things.

We went once a fortnight to visit my mother, Michael with his hair carefully parted and the sides smarmed down.

I could tell she was feeling better when she said my clothes were a disgrace and what was I doing with make-up on.

She'd been gone four months and I can't really say that I missed her. Her eyes had looked wild in the beginning, but now they took on a calm.

It was me who looked wild when I saw my reflection in the mirror.

In school they said I was very untidy and my work had gone.

Momma was due to come home the following Sunday. I spent a long time cleaning the house with Michael helping me.

You could get her some flowers from the garden, he suggested.

There were some October roses and I picked them all and filled a big vase.

We were due to go off and get Momma at about eleven. Michael was taking me, and I was going to come back with her in the doctor's car.

Will she like what we've done, do you think? I said to Michael.

He said that in his opinion she would certainly like it. The place was looking ship shape. Everything was fine.

I was coming down the stairs with my handbag, a grown-up looking thing that Michael had given me, when there was a ring at the doorbell. It was one of those old-fashioned ones you pulled, that sounded through the house.

I called to Michael to answer it, because we'd been in bed right up to the last minute, and I looked all dishevelled, and hadn't yet combed out my hair.

I tidied it quickly in the mirror and because there were voices still, murmuring, went with my bag in my hand into the hall.

The three of them standing in a circle looked up at me.

The uniforms looked oddly out of place there.

The sergeant had his hat in his hand and the constable was a woman with a mournful look to her.

Oh, I said. Oh. Is something wrong?

Michael said, Won't you go inside now Annie, I'll be in directly.

As I turned I heard the sergeant say, You'll deal with it, will you, Mr O'Shaughnessy?

I will, Sergeant. I will deal with it, Michael O'Shaughnessy said.

After a while he came into the room and sat down next to me.

You see, after all, I suppose, that we won't be going.

I see it, I said.

The scent of the roses came over me.

He said,

Annie.

I don't think I'd ever seen his hair look quite that black.

I went up to my bedroom and pinned up a quote from *Tropic of Capricorn* on the back of the door there.

O let us do some rash thing – for the sheer pleasure of it! Let us do something live and magnificent, even if destructive!

I went down to Michael and said,

Shall I get on top of you?

If you want to, Annie.

It wasn't until quite a long time later that I asked him, quite late in the evening.

Was it a stroke, or a heart-attack?

The truth of it is, he said, in his typically lyrical fashion, she hanged herself till she was dead.

O Miserere.
Miserere domine.

I held the mourning brooch in my cupped palm as though it was water.

I stood beside Michael in the front pew, entirely in black.

The scattered relatives had come from the four corners.

Good God Almighty, Michael said when he saw them. They look a lot!

His hair was flat to the sides of his head and his suit fitted.

We sang *Bread of Heaven* and I changed key for the high bits. I had to stop half way through because my voice had cracked.

Momma hadn't wanted to be cremated, so we trooped to the graveside, all of us, and watched as they lowered her in.

Michael, I said, pulling at his arm as we watched the descent of the coffin, are you sure they haven't made a mistake? Are you sure she really is dead?

I'm sure, Annie, he said, holding my elbow.

As the vicar intoned, the wind lifted his surplice. You could see the light through it, and the very fine edging of lace.

No mother could be in that box with the earth on it.

O Death, where is thy sting?

I stopped with Michael for a minute under the lych-gate.

You'll stay with me, Michael, won't you?

I'm not family, Annie. I'm not related.

You're everything, I said.

He was out of the house for the final time within a fortnight.

The lawyers had told me the executors of my mother's will were her sister Constance and a cousin by marriage called Harry Greenlove, and these two were to be appointed my guardians, to look after me and my interests until I came of age.

Constance was coming to live with me there in the house as soon as was practicable.

She was a widow, and her husband had died quite recently.

Neither she nor Harry Greenlove had been at the funeral.

He was travelling and could not be contacted.

She was ill in bed with a fever and could not attend.

They came at eleven in a large black car with a crest on the front of it.

We watched them walking across the lawn towards us and Michael said, He's a high stepping bastard and no mistake.

Constance kissed my cheek and Harry Greenlove shook my hand and then said, O'Shaughnessy. I'd like a word if you have a moment.

Constance put her hand on my shoulder and said, My dear, won't you come into the house?

In the evening Michael was there, and in the morning he was not.

Did I wake to the sound of the motor in the distance, or did I sleep through it?

I ran down the stairs and flung open the door but there was nothing left except a disturbance of air and the smell of exhaust fumes.

I saw in my head how he would have left, with the moonlight on him.

I saw him accelerating away, chasing his shadow down the empty by-ways.

There he is still, getting smaller and smaller, a pinhead.

And then there is nothing but the darkening reaches of the night.

I kept to my room most of the time, reading Miller.

Through him I was developing an interest in the major philosophers.

The guy Nietzsche, he was a real case, a case for the bug-house, I read. *And Plato wasn't such a dumb bastard, Plato had an idea or two in his bean, yes sir, yes siree. Of course, he was probably a eunuch, in those days, the big guys, the philosophers, often had their nuts cut off.*

I shied away from the parts about sex.

After Michael left I couldn't stand the eroticism.

I had learned from Henry that you could do it to your self and I did so, especially when I thought Aunt Constance might be approaching.

It gave me an extra thrill to risk getting caught.

She did nearly catch me once and came in and put her hand on my forehead and asked was I feeling all right?

I asked, had she heard from Michael?

She said she had not.

I heard her later speaking to someone on the telephone.

That Irishman. What can her mother have been thinking of? So wholly unsuitable in every respect, she said.

I was nowhere near rich but I had a comfortable independence.

My mother had left me, from Granny, more than enough to give me an education.

Cambridge, I heard Constance say to somebody.

I had decided in my own mind on Oxford.

I didn't know how, because everyone was telling me in school that my work was gone.

The thing that was worrying me most was the gravestone. I didn't know how long it would take for the earth to settle. Constance rang up the undertaker who said,

A few months.

I told her the words that I wanted, when the time came, which were a quote from Henry.

I seek, all in all, to console myself for my exile, for my exile from eternity, for that unearthing I am fond of referring to as my unheavening.

He used it, I knew even then, to justify things that he shouldn't, but I didn't care.

It isn't Romantic fancy.

The way you live, in each minute, should be shocking.

Constance said I might like to give that some thought, and consider alternatives.

In her view, less was more when it came to gravestones.

Meanwhile, she was of the opinion we should have the house redecorated and refurbished.

I told her I liked it just as it was.

She put her hand to her forehead, as if there was a pain there.

You must try to move on, Annie, she said, and put the past behind you.

Your whole past would have been forgotten had there been no memory.

I said that the house as it was, was my present, and I liked it.

The next time somebody came I listened at the door while Constance was talking.

I am trying very hard to help Annie come out of herself, I heard her saying. It's an uphill struggle, but I'm doing my best, she said.

I came down one morning to find her hanging some new curtains, on the grounds that the old ones were shabby and the whole place a disgrace.

What are these? I said as I went in and saw them.

She looked at me then with that mild look she had, quite fair and so very unlike the rest of us.

I thought that you'd like them, she said, the colours, so pretty. The old ones were morbid.

Then, changing the subject, perhaps in the hope that I might not notice,

The stone for your mother. Just her name and the dates, don't you think, Dear? And after it, *Rest in Peace.*

Peace? I shrieked, Peace? There is none. Why in God's name is anyone still pretending?

Aunt Constance walked to the window, sadly.

You're a difficult girl to fathom, Annie, she said.

A man came up from the propellant factory which was where Michael worked, to see what had become of him.

When Constance told him that Michael had gone, he said, That's a shame then. We'll miss him. O'Shaughnessy was a very good man with his hands.

One or two letters came addressed for him in writing I did not recognize, one was from Dublin, the other from Birmingham.

Constance marked them, 'Unknown Recipient' and put them back in the post-box.

I heard from Mrs Broadbent at the shop that Michael had married.

I assumed it was the woman he'd met on the ferry.

I wrote to him twice, letters of love and of longing, but didn't post them. I knew he wouldn't reply.

I lay on my bed at night and listened to the emptiness rattle in the attic.

At first I used to go up, and the smell of him lingered still, very faintly, in the room.

You know someone's gone from you when you've lost the scent of them.

It's the sound that goes next, but that's quite a long time after.

I'd search for his voice in my head, frightened, till I'd find it.

Oh God.

The time that followed was a bleak time, a bleak time indeed. A glacial time. It was a time of keen winds and no comfort. The wings of it, hovering over me, picking each minute of my living brittle and bare.

I passed myself, time and again, a little, diminishing figure.

I saw it happen, how the gap between me and myself got wider. I knew that when it was finished, I would have left myself behind.

What we put on the stone was by way of a compromise.

In my end is my beginning.

I gave in over the redecoration and Constance took me on holiday while it was done.

We went to Paris, and after I'd come down from the Eiffel Tower I sent Michael a card, to the only address I had for him, which was in Dublin.

Paris is all right, I wrote. *I wish you were with me.*

Constance said she'd had a letter from Rose at the old house, inviting us over. She hadn't told me about it before, because she thought it would upset me.

Come when you're ready. Rose had written. *Come when you want. The door is open and always will be.*

We went on a *Bateau Mouche* along the Seine. The light picked out the buildings.

A man stopped me in the *Tuileries* and said, Mon Dieu, you are so beautiful!

I wrote a few poems and threw them into the bin in my hotel bedroom. There was something about the light in Paris that I wanted to turn into words.

I opened Miller and read, *The dream was a mirage. There never was a house in the midst of the vacant lot. That's why I was never able to enter it. My home is not in this world, nor in the next. I am a monster that belongs to a reality that does not exist yet. Ah, but it does exist, it will exist, I am sure of it.*

Later that night I went out on my own. Sneaking down the stairs and past the concierge, who seemed to be sleeping.

I had Miller in my bag, a kind of talisman.

One street then another. Narrow then widening. I was walking the same streets that Miller had walked on. I knew it. I was sure of it.

I went past a bar and a girl was laughing. I wanted, with all the heart that was left to me, to be that girl. To laugh as she did.

Take it steady. Take it slow.

The voice sprung from nowhere and went straight into the centre of my head. Miller was speaking. Speaking to me. He was here, he was now. I looked around, expecting to see him beside me, feel the swish of his trench coat.

There was nothing to see, just hot air coming up in a glut of steam from a grille in the pavement, like it did in the movies.

Hell, or a film set.

You're doing OK, Miller was saying. Let's walk awhile.

I didn't have to speak. He knew all my questions.

Old Death, he was saying. You don't need to worry about him too much. Comes to us all, sooner or later. Puts his hand out. You take it, that's all. Don't have a choice, but that's neither here nor there, for now. Living's the thing – d'you see, little girl? There's so much life in you that's just busting to get out. You and me both.

We were by the river. It was flowing fast, or seemed to be, from where we were standing. I could see him now, clear but oddly super-imposed, there but not there.

Birth is behind us and death too, he was saying to me now. *Do anything, but let it yield joy. Do anything, but let it produce ecstasy.*

He was gone but the tail end of the word remained.

Ec-sta-see. A whisper that seemed to encompass everything.

I saw then that I had all I needed to become what I was, at the heart, at the core. *My language, my world, is under my arm. I am the guardian of a great secret.*

I went straight back and as soon as I got into my room sat down and wrote. I don't know what words. Words on a page, that was all that mattered. Magic. Alchemy.

The next day I woke up with the sun coming in clear through the windows. The roofs went away, to the right, to the left, their grey slates glistening.

A church bell was chiming.

I opened the window and breathed in the air, right to the bottom of my lungs and out again.

Are you ready? Constance called.

I heard Miller whisper, *It does exist. It will exist.*

I went down the stairs which seemed longer and maybe more winding than they had done

I'm ready, I said.

We stepped out together into the roaring daylight of the street.

2. HOME

SCAR TISSUE

All the way down he has been thinking of his brother. He is looking forward to seeing David. It is almost a year and that is the longest they have been apart. When their mother left them for a time all those years ago, just kids actually, they sliced the skin on each others wrists with a kitchen knife and pressed the cuts close so the blood mingled. It was David, ever the practical one, who pointed out that there wasn't any need, for they shared after all the same blood, having come out together, not all that many minutes apart, through the same orifice. That bloody journey from dark to light is something they know they have in common, have always known, but do not speak about. They drifted apart somewhat after puberty. But the scars have remained, they have made a joke about that sometimes. David is a doer, the mother has said. But John – ah, he is the one with his head in the clouds.

Coming out of Birmingham the train has been slow, a fault on the points near New Street station. A girl across the carriage smiles and he smiles back before retreating. A book in his hand. He is studying philosophy and is now on Nietzsche. He doesn't rate him. God is dead! Pity is useless! He and David agreed years ago they were not believers. It stood to reason – it does still stand – that the prayers they sent up every night, kneeling by their beds in the cold old house while their father wept and their mother was elsewhere – Please send her back, God! Send her back to us! – those prayers would have been answered, and the mother would have returned, right then and there, and they would have reverted to being a family, had there been, as there was supposed to be, a listening God.

He has been in the city without leaving it since February, and it is now December. The long, hot Summer when you could feel the pavements burning up through the soles of your feet is just a memory. In that heat he saw the buildings themselves jump and shiver. When the bell sounded from St Barnabas church on the top of the hill the notes that came out were bent sideways. The nights were still, and the heated-up air hung above you like a blanket. He forgot then, if he ever knew it, how you could breathe.

It is different now. They are in the grip of what some people say is the worst freeze for thirty years. The fields of Worcestershire are whipping by the train like plates of steel. The sky is slate-grey. No compromise. Now it is Ledbury and the train empties. My summit is before me! He has been reading his Nietzsche slowly. *My highest mountain, and after it, my abyss.*

He has not heard from his brother in some time, but that does not surprise him. David has never had the inclination for writing. Occasionally a note, or a card sometimes, 'Isle of Man TT' (a phase when he was into motorbikes). Or once a postcard with an image of a Bazaar on the front, 'It's hot in Tunisia'. Their mother's letters have kept them in touch. She writes every week with news of the life in the small market town, divorces, babies, deaths, entrances. How business in the shop (they run a small general store cum tobacconist) has slowed considerably since last season. How David will find a niche for himself soon, surely. But meanwhile – does not John think so? – perhaps it is a blessing to have him there with them at home.

When he steps onto the platform at Hereford station he is struck by the fact that the air is different. Damp and leafy and coming from somewhere he used to know well, but does no longer. He stands for a minute after the guard has waved the train off and looks along the empty tracks and then up and down the emptier platform.

'Wellspring'. The word has come into his head. He takes out his notebook and jots it down. It must and will have relevance to something. Everything has relevance to everything else. He and David talked about this a lot in the old days. Nobody in the world exists alone, everyone, everywhere is part of a system. A check over here and a balance over there but the system is stable. OK brother? They each breathed a sigh. They still both believed it. OK brother. It was on this basis that they both went forward in the world.

The bus from Hereford seems to travel incredibly slowly. He takes out his mother's last letter from his inside pocket. It is worn at the creases with folding and unfolding. No mention of David. No mention of anything, beyond the mundane. The omission seems stranger, the harder he looks. The absence more yawning, the closer he approaches.

It is gone three thirty by the time he gets off in Abergavenny. There is a market on, with Christmas coming the town is busy, tinsel everywhere, and bundled up in navy blue overcoats, a wheezy band of the Salvation Army. Without knowing why, he throws in a coin and averts his gaze from the lit-up Christmas tree. Too garish by far. The side streets are better, darker and quieter. He turns off into them, and with just a few people coming and going, makes his way in the familiar direction.

The house looks the same although he thought there would be more light in the windows. It is a terrace and his mother has always hated it. For the whole of his life she has wanted a detached house, a proper house, a house with more room, so she could feel at home in it.

Out of our league. His father has said that. Over and over. But still, she has hankered. It was that, she has said, the wanting and wanting – hope, was it? – that drove her, all those years ago, to the brink.

That was what she has told them anyway, in her bad moments. Those moments have got fewer as she has grown older and have never been as bad as when she was sent away from the place. How small they both were. They watched her go. She did not go far, but it might as well have been to the other side of the moon, from all she said when she at last returned to them. Like Hell only worse. That is what she said.

Pen y Fal. The loony bin, some people called it. He and David used to creep over there and keep watch. The perimeter was fenced with a high link fence with barbed wire on top and a metal overhang.

Keep Out, the sign said.

A double lattice. A thousand linkages. And the great brick building with its high chimneys that was once a country house and now had the look of something distinctly less salubrious. The windows seemed almost to bend outwards with the pressure of whatever was festering inside them. *Let me out! Let me out!*

Wake up, John.

There would be David, shaking his shoulder.

I'm scared, David.

There's nothing to be scared of. Go back to sleep.

The day he and David decided they would go and look for their mother they hung about by the fence. *D'you think she'll come out? I don't know. I don't know.* All they saw was an old crone behind a hedge who waved her arms and screamed something. A nurse came out running and herded her in, then came across and told them they should leave that place, that it was wicked to stand there, taunting and grinning.

David was smiling. He saw it then, a smile like none before or since, a peculiar smile with his lips half sideways. *Come on David.* A hand on the wrist. David looking like himself again. *Let's get out of here.*

When their mother came home she said the currents of electricity they put through your head turned you into someone else. No memory. All gone. The smiles. The tears.

And without that, what are you? Over and over. *I ask you, what are you?*

Together on the sofa, he and David, shrinking away from her. That flesh. Was the electricity in it still? Please don't touch me.

Their father standing by. *Hush now.* His hands were hopeless.

The mother did not speak of it again, or only rarely. Over time, bit by bit, the elements of herself that had been distributed to the four corners reassembled. On the rare occasions she did speak, it was of something experienced at a distance. Those times? Oh yes. They were Hell, surely. Like a heat wave almost forgotten after the first rain.

The streetlight just outside the house is stuttering and blinking. John rings the bell, he does not know why, it seems appropriate. The house is looking bald and bare with its curtains drawn and no chink anywhere of an open window. Is that a sound? Nobody comes. The cold takes hold of him, and a bitter current of icy air comes up the street and pinches his ears and his fingers in their gloves. His bag is a cold weight on his shoulder, his things for staying the week inside it, and a few presents, not wrapped yet, for his mother and father, and for David a copy of an old *Dan Dare* annual that he picked up in a second hand bookshop. David has always been a sucker for those old tales. Life on Mars. Journey into Space. The exploits of Doc and Lemmie Caution. Innocence, is it? The age they grew up in. Conquering the world and what was beyond it still possible.

The bolt now is sliding back slowly. Oh John, it is you. A whisper only. His mother? Really?

His father behind her. You're back then, Son. The hand held out, the fingers shaking.

Hot. The room. Stifling, actually. How can they breathe?

His mother rattling china cups on the kitchen counter. The kettle rumbling.

How have you been? Turning to the father. And where is David?

The knuckles of the old man's hand are taut and showing whitely.

Mum? Going into the kitchen now. Where's David?

Tears, tears running down her cheeks and under her chin, and wetting the neckline of her blouse – dirt is it? Around the neck?

He goes up the steep stairs two at a time. David's room is on the top floor landing. That smell – what is it? Incense? Or? Another world, not one he knows.

David? Knocking at the door, knuckles of his first and second finger, rat-tat-tat, rat-tat-tat. The code. The old code. *Friend. Brother.*

The handle turning slowly now. The door swings back. Swings wide. Too wide.

And David. Yes. His brother. There?

The bright red crucifix, man high. Blocked in. Magenta. Scarlet. Blood-red.

David? It's me?

The head lolls forward, tongue slopped out. The careful coronet of holly, pricked into the scalp. A man on tiptoe, arms spread wide. Christ. I am Christ! Three drops of blood, all three dried now, spattering the forehead. Next to the eye, a longer streak, running down, running sideways.

Born again, the words come out. In this world to be your saviour. David. No. It's John. It's John.

You who have blessed me, I will succour you. You who have cursed me, I will be your friend.

The sleeve up now, the wrist, the scar.

We made a pact. For God's sake, David. Look here. Blood brothers. You and me. The knife. The cut. Remember it?

David is smiling at him now, like an older brother, bigger and stronger and just ahead, like he has been throughout the time from then to now, and will be always. Surely. Surely?

I am your brother, and your father too. David is saying, his smile all sideways, like it was that day at Pen y Fal when the crone shouted.

I am the resurrection and the life.

His hands. What now? He holds them out. Stigmata, yes. From palm to back. Implanted through. As clear as day. And on the feet and at the side. A gash half healed. Mother of God. *If I should die before I wake.*

Blood brothers! What is there to know of these new marks, of this new blood? Nothing. There is just a huge surprise. Nothing of death or life either. Pity. Compassion. God. Love. If David is Christ, then he is nothing. Nothing surely. He is a boy no longer. He is a man only.

The quiet looking ambulance has taken David. Dawn has come and gone already. They are not allowed to see him for a week, it is better that way, so the doctor said. Time can be a great healer.

His mother has bought out a Christmas tree, only a small one, and put ribbons on it. More tasteful, she says, under the circumstances, than shiny ornaments.

His parents appear to like their presents, scented soaps for his mother, and for his father, a striped tie.

At the dinner table they raise a glass. To David's health. To their own also. His mother wonders whether perhaps it runs in the family. But John – it will never affect John. Never in this world. He is the one with his feet on the ground. John – he is their mainstay, surely.

In the cellar he finds some magnolia emulsion which he takes up to paint over the crucifix. It takes three coats and even after he has finished that, there is still the shadow of the cross visible.

He tells his mother he is going to take the *Dan Dare* annual over to Pen y Fal, so that David can have it on Christmas Day, if he is well enough.

His mother observes that David always did love exploring.

After they have listened to the Queen's Speech he sets out to walk along the old path to the perimeter. If it is not the same fence it is practically a replica. But bigger, stronger. Ice has gathered thick in the linkages and the wind is whistling through in a singing sound.

Praise. Is that it?

The lights are coming on in the many windows of that place and as he is watching they surge then go out and then came on again. All the tender elements of his brother's brain being blown apart. Can that be happening? Now? At this instant? Their shared memories fizzled to nothing on a bolt of electricity? *God is dead.*

The lights in the building burn steadily again. Behind one of those windows his brother is, asleep or awake, it makes no difference.

He pushes back his sleeve and feels on his wrist for the familiar shape of the old scar he made with David. *Blood Brothers. Till the end of time.*

There is no mark there. The flesh is smooth. Perhaps there has never been a mark. In this world of illusion, anything is possible.

He is sure he can hear 'The First Noel' coming across the cold air, faintly.

The *Dan Dare* annual is weighing now in his pocket heavily. He takes it out and positions it carefully against the fence. It looks quite like some kind of offering, a wreath you lay on Remembrance Sunday.

Sleep tight, brother.

He hears a voice whispering in his head something that sounds like *Lemmie Caution.*

Above him the cloud is torn apart and the moon is allowed to show itself briefly.

He is breathing now, breathing more deeply than he ever has done.

Everything is related to everything else. Love. Loss. Hope. Memory.

He can see the lights at the edge of the town, there, beckoning. Just a few paces and he'll be back on asphalt. Ordinary streets. Ordinary people.

The wind comes up and touches his cheek with any icy finger. When he looks back, the lit windows of Pen y Fal are no longer visible. He doesn't ask why, doesn't think at all. He turns up his coat collar, shrugs his body down into his jacket, takes a first step on the path that leads towards home.

SPECIAL

It wasn't that you went for the bad boys, but they were the only ones available. The proper boys, the ones that were still at school and wore caps and blazers, they didn't count. The boys that lived down over the bridge in the crappy houses, that you weren't supposed to have anything to do with – they were men, not boys. Men, with all that implied and suggested. That was the secret.

You were working at the milk bar on Sundays when the one came in that you'd been watching out of the corners of your eyes. Muscles, certainly. A kind of swagger that suggested a pay packet at the end of each week. He ordered a coffee and you made it strong, two spoonsful of Nescafé, and watched it fizzle as you poured on the boiling water.

You make it like that for the boys off the road, Mr Hanbury had said. He was the proprietor, a man with his bottom much too close to the ground. His wife was taller and quite beautiful. It was said she'd got in the family way with the son of one of the toffs in the area. Hanbury was bribed to marry her as part of the pay off, you'd heard your father saying to your mother. Well, there you are, you see, your mother replied.

Your father didn't like you working in the milk bar. He'd said so once and then let it be. Your mother said nothing for she was dead by that time. It all happened quickly. You heard there was a job going on Sundays and offered yourself. Just gone up and done it, spoken to short little Hanbury in person. He'd looked you up and down for a moment. Asked what did your father think. When you'd said it was up to you to decide, he'd looked down his nose, and said you were probably too posh for the position. But something – what was it? made him think again. We can try it anyway, he'd said then. Give it a go, if you're not afraid of hard work.

The work wasn't that hard. You had to keep the counter clean and the nozzles all wiped and the bottles tidy. Otherwise they'd have the Food Standards all over them, Mr Hanbury said. Mrs Hanbury came sometimes with her pleasantly calm and unfocused look and didn't say anything. Except once she asked if you could make your skirts a bit longer. When you bend over to reach the low cartons I can see your stocking tops, was what she said. That made you feel peculiar, somehow. Your stocking tops were, after all, your own business. And you could see in your head your mother still doing hers up as she'd used to. Bending and straightening, adjusting the seams at the back with care, it was only the common women who couldn't be bothered to keep their seams straight. Slatternly, that was it. And your mother was sure that with the upbringing you had, and the proper breeding, and the best schooling, you'd never find you wanted to grow up like that.

He came in, young Duggie, the worst of that bunch from down over the bridge. A poor part of town, not one where people would care to live if they had the option. But needs must, your father said quite often. And it takes all sorts. You wondered whether his attitude might have mellowed somewhat, on the grounds that he – and you by default, that was inescapable – had, in some slip of fate that was hard to account for, been coming down in the world for quite a long time now.

Debt comes to all of us, Mr Hanbury said. But then again, it comes more to some than to others.

Was there a covert criticism in his words? A criticism of your father and you and all that you stood for? A criticism even of your poor late mother, who shouldn't have gone and died like she did?

Duggie came in and drank his strong coffee and sat on the stool on the other side of the counter, astride like all that crowd of boys did, the men-boys, the misfits, like they were riding the motorbikes they couldn't afford but would do one day, yes, as long as the pay packets kept rolling in and they didn't go and get some young floozy up the spout, with a baby in no time and National Assistance down the line.

He was watching you, Duggie, while appearing not to. It came to you then that perhaps he was shy. *Diffident* – that was the word you much preferred. For you were into words in a big way even then. Their subtle distinctions. Their pains and their pleasures. The way nothing could give you the thrill a word could, laid out on the page for your delectation. Your friend. Your adversary.

Duggie was watching as you reached and bent forward. Up to the top of the highest shelf then down to the bottom-most rung of the arrangement.

A place for everything and everything in its place, was Mr Hanbury's dictum. A pompous little bugger, old Hanbury, had been your mother's opinion. Your father felt that the Hanburys of this world were all well and good so long as they made sure not to overstep any boundaries.

A common little man, poor Hanbury, with next to no education. But he's done well for himself.

Was there envy in that? A kind of despair? The bills were coming in thick and fast, that much you were sure of. They piled up on the window sill in the breakfast room and dust accumulated. There had to be an opening and a reckoning somewhere not too far down the line.

Duggie sat on the stool on the other side of the bar and watched and watched you. He didn't say anything. You'd heard him speak once or twice and it was mostly monosyllables. The other boy-men steered clear of him. Respect or fear, you couldn't be sure which it was, but Duggie was top dog, there was no doubt about it. And something about his being top dog made you look at him hard. Made a warm kind of feeling come up from somewhere.

Is your coffee all right?

It's fine. Coffee's fine.

He slurped a little bit and the coffee spilled over the sides of the cup as he put it down. Were his hands shaking? When you looked at his hands you could see the fingers were evenly spaced and the knuckles strong. Kind hands, was the thought that came into your head. Hands certainly that made and shaped things.

There was no one at all at the counter or in the lower seating area when four o'clock came. How long was it Duggie had been there? Ages and ages. The afternoon was hot and slow and in the far window that overlooked where the street bent around and just beyond that the steps to the church with the gravestones leaning, flies were buzzing up lazily against the glass.

What was he saying to you? What time did you finish? But he knew that already. Could he walk you home? To the bus? To your gate? Could he walk you anywhere?

What was it about him that you perceived then? I'm not asking, his look and his manner seemed to say. He hitched his belt up and stood with his feet planted quite far apart, like the cowboys did in the Westerns on television. Not that you watched the television very much. It had only been got in for the sake of your mother. In those last days when she couldn't bear to think of anything. The next best thing to a drug, the television, your father said. Watch too much of it and it'll eat away at your mind.

At a quarter past five Mr Hanbury came and said you could go, he'd lock the place up. There wasn't much doing on a Sunday evening. People getting ready for the working week that was just ahead of them. The last buses leaving early out of the town.

Did he look at you oddly? A look that said, I know the type. Supposed to be posh but when you scratch the surface, no better than she should be.

The street was quite hot still, the late sun reflecting off the buildings both sides. It was hard to breathe in how you usually did. And you found, to your surprise almost, that it was equally difficult the breathe out again.

Duggie was waiting. Thirty five minutes to your last bus. He walked you down to Chippenham Meade and under the trees where the shade was falling. The river ran slowly, the Wye it was, that your father had once owned lots and lots of, miles and miles, both banks, yes, those were the good times.

D'you fish? Duggie said. I'll take you fishing.

You said you didn't know how to fish and he said there was

nothing at all to it, the daft little buggers snapped up the hook and that was that.

Hook, line and sinker. Where did that thought come from?

Duggie kissed you out of sight behind a tree trunk. He smelled of something cheap and sweet. That was your first thought. Your second was, is this how kisses are supposed to taste? A bit sour, and gloopy? You felt his tongue then, trying to push in between your teeth. Quite big and meaty and covered in a spittle that was not your spittle.

That's all right, Duggie said. I won't go too fast. You're special, see?

You had to run for the bus and he ran with you. Were you surprised when he got on too? Paid both the fares, one and a half, because you still got charged the fare for children.

Under sixteen, is it? Duggie said, and grinned quietly.

You thought your father might notice something but when you got in he seemed preoccupied. He had something to tell you, something that didn't reflect very well on him or the family.

What did you do?

It was more, he said, what he hadn't done, and therein lay the problem. The National Insurance for the men he'd employed – he hadn't been paying it.

It's a court case I'm afraid. I'll plead guilty. An unfortunate oversight. Extenuating circumstances. Your mother's illness.

But it was likely, he said, to be in the paper. People would talk. It would all blow over, of course it would. You should take no notice. Head held high – that was his motto.

You didn't think at the time he was crying. Only long afterwards that thought came to you. All you saw then, and weren't sure how to interpret it, was he stopped speaking and put his head in his hands.

The time between that Sunday and the next went slowly. On the Tuesday your father dressed up in his best and went off to court, and the report of the case attracted a paragraph in the local paper. As you watched him go off you saw for the first time his suit was not like the suits of other men. It looked like those ones you saw in old films from before the war, gangster movies, Al Capone, with the shoulders padded out and wide lapels and the turn ups flapping around his ankles.

Mr Hanbury looked at you sideways when you got to the milk bar at ten o'clock. His wife came and hovered and patted your shoulder and then went away again. A girl needs a mother, was all she said. The paper with the report in was up in the rack but nobody took it down to read it. Old news already, Hanbury said, wiping the counter.

The milk bar was quiet, unusually so. Were people staying away deliberately? Not wanting to be served by you? Your father's daughter? Up in court? In the papers? Fined and bound over?

Duggie didn't come in. Mr Hanbury said, I see your admirer's left you in the lurch.

You thought he wouldn't be waiting for you when you came out.

But he was there, at the end of the street, leaning against the wall of a building, smoking and with a look on his face that you took to be smiling.

You didn't speak at all, going down to Chippenham Meade. It was peaceful somehow. He held your hand and his skin was very dry and warm which was reassuring.

You don't need to worry about the bus, he said. I've borrowed a car.

You lay down by the river. There was no one about. A swan went by and you said to Duggie that kings in the past used to eat swan, it was regarded as a delicacy.

His forehead wrinkled up then and he stared into the distance. His eyes were pale blue, rather watery, and you couldn't tell whether they had any depth to them.

You're special, you are, was what he said.

He kissed you the way he had done before and this time you let him put his tongue in. When you felt his hand on your knee first of all and then inching up above your stocking tops, you thought of your mother saying, Don't let a man touch your nether regions. If a man tries to do that, he's up to no good.

Duggie was rubbing himself against you, soft and then hard.

You told him to stop and he did so immediately. Lay on his back and stared up at the sky, breathing, breathing.

I see your old man's been had up, he said.

Shut up, shut up, shut up, shut up.

Was it really you shouting? The tears too – were they your tears? Wet on your face with him wiping them off with the flat of his fingers. Rough at the sides like emery paper.

I'll take you home.

When he got to the turn to your house he went past.

D'you like the car? We can go for a drive.

Up the lane, around the bend. Just a mile beyond where the woodlands began he drove off onto a hard cored track and pulled up the car in a grassy clearing. The silence when you got out was extremely intense. Just a few birds calling. Evening, that was it. The shadows laid out like pointing fingers.

We won't stay long. But your old man won't trouble. Things on his mind.

The grass was soft. You thought his eyelashes were a bit like butterflies' wings and you leaned in and kissed them. He held you up to him and whispered, You're special. Ain't seen a girl as special as you. Never. No way.

Were you? Was that it? You'd always been led to believe it was so, but not like this, not in the way that Duggie meant it.

Your knickers on the grass, his hips first heavy then light then heavy again.

The surprise of that entry would never go away in all the years afterwards.

Christ! He cried out then.

It was dusk when he dropped you outside the house. A single light shone from the front hallway.

Dad? You called out.

Duggie hadn't kissed you goodbye, had barely spoken.

Next week? you'd half whispered. Did he answer? Hard to say.

The car drove off quickly. You could tell by the revs when he got to the junction he didn't use the brakes.

Dad?

He was in the breakfast room with papers of all shapes and sizes in piles around him. A bin at his feet held the torn up envelopes. From the dresser your mother was looking on, in that photograph both alive and younger.

Thought I'd better do some clearing out. There's a lot to catch up with.

His voice didn't sound a bit like him. Smaller. Weaker.

There's an awful lot here. I don't know. I can't tell.

Your mother was looking at the new you, the old him. What was that look? Ironic? Disapproving? Or merely neutral, as befits, you have come to see lately, both the long- and the rather more newly-dead.

You're late, aren't you?

He's getting up now.

Did Hanbury ask you to work overtime?

He's stopping, next to you. Can he hear your heart beating? Duh duh duh duh duh duh duh duh. Fast and furious.

Your mother is watching over his shoulder. I know you, she is saying, I know both of you.

His hand on your arm.

You're all right, aren't you? You like working there?

He's walking out with you, out of the room, she's watching, she's calling, Are your seams straight? Are you my own daughter?

Hanbury is lucky to have you of course, your father is saying. A girl like you. He won't get a chance like that every day.

He's closing the door now, ushering you out before him, into the rest of the house. Your house. Your future.

Enterprising little man, Hanbury. Got his head screwed on. Knows the genuine article when he sees it.

You catch your mother's eye one last time. It's not her. She's gone. It's a photograph of someone who's dead. That's it. That's all.

The latch drops and the door clicks to behind you.

A man like Hanbury, your father says. I shouldn't be surprised if Hanbury were to go a long way.

Waiting Room

When we set off for the doctor's surgery I sit beside my mother in the car, holding the book in my hand for comfort as I have been doing for quite some time now, ever since I found it on the side table in the dark little room where my brother had been lying, the very night that his coffin had gone from it, late, it was late already and a full moon.

I sit beside my mother in the back seat with the doctor driving, and us behind him like he was a chauffeur, and he is speaking to my mother, speaking all the time to her quietly, in the kind of slow voice he has used to me sometimes, with his hand on my forehead to check how hot I am, or the cold end of the stethoscope slipping through the slit where my nightie falls open, just at the soft part that starts at the base of the throat.

Evie will be all right, don't you worry about that, he says. The important thing is to get you better, don't you think Mrs Maloney, getting better is the main thing, and everything back to normal after, everything shipshape.

He takes the big double bends at the wrong angle and everything tilts sideways, the adverse camber can do that to you, and my mother holds onto my hand as if doing so could prevent her from falling, and then it is over, that moment, and the car rocks back to the centrifuge of its own suspension, and the hedges return to the height they should be, and my mother says, If you say so, doctor, and looks out over the fields either side of us, and the fields are reflected back on themselves, like the sky is, in her eyes, in their pale grey colour that is shrinking and expanding.

By the time we arrive at the outskirts of the town, having crossed the river by the narrow stone bridge where she used to take us, my brother and me, to bathe on the good days when summer had come and the evenings were still long and the sun had not gone behind a single cloud for the whole duration of the time that was measurable, by the time that occurs my mother has gone off again.

What is that noise now? She says. That noise like a bell. Oh stop it doctor, stop the bell tolling.

I can see how he looks at her then, his eyes in the mirror, the mirror itself like a visor with just his eyes showing, and I cannot quite tell what expression is in them, puzzlement maybe, or sorrow, or boredom, or some other emotion that I cannot access, and then with surprising suddenness we are there and he pulls the car up and says, Wait for a minute, and switches off the engine and goes in to the place marked 'Surgery', by the side door.

It is market day and the town is quite full and I can hear the cattle lowing in their pens to share the information that death is approaching. At the top of the town by the river is the slaughterhouse and at the end of a busy day there, you will see the blood running in the gutters and the men with brooms sluicing it with water and sweeping down after it. On those kind of days in the afternoons it is peculiarly silent. It is as if a spell of silence has come over the town.

Well, here we are then, my mother says, in a voice that to all intents and purposes is normal.

But I am not to be led astray by its apparent normality, so I open my book, and immediately enter the world of the words that I can get lost in, one word then another, *if, and, but, how*, the spaces and conjunctions, the rises and falls, the gaps that you find that are like a precipice.

Will you read me a bit, my mother says then, just a line or two Evie. You know how it soothes me.

The lines on the page are as follows, the start of the book that I have not read yet:

Once you have given up the ghost, everything follows with dead certainty.

I know the word 'dead' is not one my mother will relish, so I make up the start of the book in a way that I think may appeal and will calm her:

At half past six the man came out of the house wearing a turban and with bare feet though the day was a cold one.

Ah, that is a good start, my mother says. That sounds like a story. Hearing a story always takes me out of myself.

He did not notice at first there was snow on the ground, for the cold did not reach him. It was getting quite dark and the clock chimed the quarter and the wind began rising.

The doctor appears by the side of the car. He has not come back out through the door, he has come by another direction, and I do not understand that, for the side door is the one you go in and out of, it has been that way always, ever since we first started coming, on the fortnightly visits which then became weekly, and became, in the end, or maybe the beginning, the fulcrum, the focus, the one single element in all that there was that would surely save us, the ring that is tossed on the waters when they get too much for you, the promise of calm in the tumult that was our house.

Will you come with me now, Mrs Maloney, the doctor says. And you can come too, Evie, and wait in the waiting room.

There is no one today in that room that is quite like a drawing room with chintz curtains. Four doors lead off from it, one you can see has been made quite newly.

It's a pity you ruined this room with your alterations, doctor, my mother says to him.

Ah well now, he says, it's progress you see, Mrs Maloney. Things move on They have to.

The receptionist comes forward and takes my mother by the arm, and they go, with her on one side and the doctor on the other, out through the new door, around which the plaster is still settling, and the black latch closes behind them with a click.

To want to change the condition of things seemed futile to me; nothing would be altered.

The book is light in my hand, but heavier than its meaning.

Its meaning takes shape in my head like a feather, or the merest brush stroke.

I quickly saw the contradiction between the real and the unreal. I had need of nobody.

The side door opens and a draught comes in that brings up goose pimples on my arm in a pattern.

If it isn't young Evie, a voice says then, and I see the black turn ups of the Reverend's trousers, then the pleats at the waistband, then the belt straining.

His wife is next to him and she leans towards me.

And how is your dear mother? What a shock that was, with the poor boy going.

I see the expression then that they both had, the night that it happened, the planes of their faces picked out clearly, the lights in the windows and the darkness outside them, and the look that they had as they drew me towards them, that was not satisfaction but was right next door to it.

They go over to speak to the receptionist who has come back in, but I cannot hear much, for they are speaking in that peculiar under voice that is not quite a whisper but is aiming to be so.

Some words come up to me, though. Shame. Accidental. Concern. Negligent.

They all look over towards me then, so I hold the book up like a shield between us.

You don't have to think it was your fault, Evie, the Reverend says.

The lines on the page are blurring together.

Who could change the hearts of men?

The receptionist says, An inch or two deep. Who would have thought it.

Right on cue a cry comes up from the back room, a long drawn out No-oooh-ooh with a sound at the end of it like glass breaking.

It's the grief that does it, the Reverend's wife says.

I block out the sound by concentrating hard on the words in front of me, *chaos, need, jangle, discord.*

The room seems suddenly to me then like a stage set, with noises off, a cry, a whimper.

From the very beginning I trained myself not to need anything too badly.

I'm here, Evie, in my official capacity, the Reverend says.

He is coming towards me. He looks like an uncle, but then not quite so.

I'm here to see everything right and tight, to see you're looked after, but there's nothing to be afraid of.

He takes hold of my arm and I feel through the thinnish material of my blouse the heat of his skin, just as I remembered it.

You'll be coming to stay with us for a while. You'll like that, won't you?

Of course she will like it, his wife says. She used to like coming. Didn't you, Evie?

The receptionist from behind her desk is looking on, and mouthing some word that looks like generosity.

I read in the book, *Though I was weaned young, the poison never left my system.*

Forgiveness, now, Evie, there is the thing, the Reverend is saying. We should all seek forgiveness.

A bullock that has broken out of his pen charges past the window with a piercing bellow and at exactly that moment my mother lets out a scream and goes on screaming.

The moment anything was demanded of me, I balked.

A sudden silence descends on the room, profound and total. It is the silence, surely, that you get before words and then get again after them.

The Reverend has some papers in his hand, is folding them up, says, You're coming home with us now.

I close the book then and hold it to my chest with my both arms folded.

Are you listening, Evie? Will you at least not answer?

The doctor comes out, on his own, lacing his hands in a washing movement.

The plaster round the door looks rough at the edges like an unhealed wound does.

Your mother needs treatment, Evie, he says. We'll see that she gets it.

She told me to watch him, I say then. She asked me. I was reading.

I see once again my brother's face in the water, so pale, so unlike him.

The Reverend's wife says, It was too much to ask.

The doctor says, It was too much, all of it.

My mother comes out looking quite like my mother but not wholly.

They'll pack up your things, so they said, she says to me. You won't mind going to the Reverend, will you?

I can see from the corner of my eye through the window the bullock being led back into his pen with a man either side of him.

I tell her I won't mind.

It is time now, the doctor says, but my mother does not move straight away, instead she says, as though nobody else in the world existed, Will you tell me again how it started, Evie? How the story started?

At half past six, I recite from my head, *the man came out of the house wearing a turban and with bare feet though the day was a cold one.*

Ah that is a good start, the Reverend's wife says. That sounds like a story.

A black car pulls up and the doctor says, Here we are, then, and my mother steps forward.

That's not how it starts, I say to her then. It isn't the story.

She kisses me once on the forehead, in the old way, and what I see next is her back in the doorway and the car door opening, then the doctor getting in next to her.

The Reverend and his wife come and stand either side of me.

It was getting quite dark and the clock chimed the quarter and the wind began rising.

Give us that book, Evie. We will look after it.

The car pulls away and I see what might be my mother's face going by in a blur as she looks back out at me.

Do you hear me, Evie?

The room is silent but in my head there is a clock chiming.

In the Reverend's hand the book looks small and very insubstantial.

There was snow on the ground.

How bitter that wind is! How icy the man's feet are!

The Reverend's wife says, The girl is shivering.

The man looks at me and I look back at him.

In that cold night of stars we regard each other across tractless millennia.

The Reverend puts his hand on my shoulder and tightens his fingers while his wife smiles a little round 'o' that puckers her lipstick in a kiss-like travesty.

Hush! That wind. Can you hear it blowing from the far side of time?

The Reverend on one side, his wife on the other, we move to the door where the doctor is waiting, next to the receptionist.

You'll be all right, will you, Evie?

In the snow and the wind the man shrugs his shoulders and opens his palms like they had nothing in them.

Here we are, his look seems to say, You and I. Here we always will be.

I'm here if you need me, the doctor says.

And before I know it, the door to the waiting room has clicked to behind us.

The Reverend and his wife are propelling me forwards.

The car door is open.

I can smell the stale smell of that old interior, a smell like sickness or cow's intestines.

In my head the wind drops and the night is empty.

The snow has no footprints.

But the house in that vista of darkness is lit up, in its windows a warmth that I know must reside there. The man is inside and has taken off his turban. His dark hair is flowing in thick locks on his shoulders. In his pale feet the veins are restoring the heat and the coals on the fire are burning up with a yellow intensity.

Get in now, Evie.

The Reverend is driving, with his wife beside him.

He turns on the ignition and the headlights flare up with a strange new clarity.

The church clock chimes once and we all hear it.

As the engine turns over the Reverend says, It's going to be a cold night.

THE RETURNING

He hasn't been back for a very long time but even so he expects the landmarks to look more familiar. Here is the bend in the road ahead of him. But is it the right one? Is his bend farther on – the bend he braced himself for every morning, tightening his knees as the bus swung into it, clenching his back against the camber, then suddenly balanced again and cresting the rise?

And here is the town. It was the right bend, the last bend before the straight takes hold of you. Ahead now the spire of St Mary's church in the middle distance. What is it he feels? An itch? An excitement? Perhaps what he feels is actually nothing at all.

There is no one to meet him. The email dashed off at the last minute to the son of a cousin bounced back to him. Account Closed, was the message. It was right. It was fitting. It gives him, or at least he likes to think so, a sense of freedom. Of no obligation. Of being able to do exactly what he wants to in the world.

But still, as he gets off the bus in what used to be the old Bus Station, he feels an aloneness. How it used to be. How the crowds would part as the buses eased out into the street, one after another. How the stench of dung coming in from the market over the hot pavement caught at your throat. How you heard the background rise up then, cattle and sheep and pigs and chickens, in the heart, in the head. An exhaust back-firing.

Today it is quiet. The streets are clean – just a few of yesterday's lottery tickets discarded here and there, a sweet wrapper, a cigarette end by itself in the gutter. Just a smart land cruiser pulling off from the kerb, its exhaust muted.

He has no plan. The idea of this visit, at first no more than a little knocking in the back of his brain, has come out of nowhere. There is no anniversary. No need. No reason.

And yet here he is, in the street, in the air. Familiar, is it? Different? His old air?

The shops – little gifts that nobody in their right mind could want. Banks of soaps and scents in multi coloured wrappings. Ribbons. Candles. Cushions. Gewgaws.

Now a coffee house – no, two. No, three, actually. Estate Agents – there in their branded liveries. *Desirable Residence. Newly Renovated.*

Now the restaurants – *Samphire: Exotic Cuisine. Ho-Pac Takeaway. Posh Fish.* Then, an anomaly, *Archie's Kebab House,* next to what looks like a funeral parlour.

No sign of a grocer. Just the chain offerings. *Simply Food. Waitrose.*

The street rises slightly under his feet. This is the place – isn't it? Where the pavements narrow and the buildings come in? Then farther on – Agincourt Square. The Shire Hall. The statue of Rolls with a bi-plane balanced in the palm of his hand. Henry V overlooking it all. The cobblestones. The arches.

This is the place – yes. The shop front still there, the modest expanse of glass and old wood with the paint peeling.

The name – has it gone? There is no awning. But up at the top, the letters still show in ghost fashion. *Sterret's Bakery.*

The smell of fresh bread coming out of the ovens rushes in and assails him.

He is ten, he is five, he is nothing at all.

On the first floor above him, a window opens.

You're early, aren't you? Mr – Andrews, is it? Wait. I'll come down.

The window clicks to before he can answer. Then steps on the stairs, somewhere deep in the interior.

When the door opens up – who is it? Who is she? No-one he knows? A woman with a wisp of pale hair coming down from a badly-done bun. A blouse on, with buttons at the top quite askew. As though she has been blasted by a high wind, though there is no movement anywhere, no breath or abatement.

You've come then, at last. You'd better come in.

She steps back and gestures.

And then he is in, in there again. Is it as he remembered? The counter – it was on the left surely?

It's in a bit of a mess, the woman is saying. Has been for a long time. But if you should want to take it, it's yours, for the right rental.

He opens his mouth to explain, to account. *I am not Mr Andrews. I am –* . Who? That question. But she is already expounding how, with a little ingenuity much may be done. All you need is the money. And the will, certainly.

For the town is booming – has he not seen it? New people coming in. It was the roads that did it, then the bridge, gradually. Now people commuting. To Bristol. To Gloucester. Some even taking the train, she is saying, from Newport to London. People like lawyers or graphic designers. It is the new way, certainly. But it does leave a gap, in the week, in the daytime. Like the heart of something has been ripped out. When you walk up the street it feels like there is a hole in the town.

She is on the top step, and the little, cramped landing is as he remembered it.

As he draws level, she holds her hand out.

I'm Anne Sterret, by the way. Not that it matters to anyone now, but I was born here.

He sees it now, sees her for the first time as she is, as she was.

Should he say it? Admit? Say, Don't you remember? Speak the words that would bring up the ghosts from the myriad places they are hiding – or resting, is it?

He says nothing, just makes some small sound that might be polite acknowledgement, and in any case she has opened the door, opened it already to the interior that he knows, in that instant, is what he has come for.

There it is, with the light as it always has been, coming in through the high window facing the south, and the town, overlooking it. From here you can see – what is it, precisely? Everything and nothing. The roofs of the houses going away, the streets and the chimneys, the glint of the river caught in its bend around Chippenham Mead, the lean of the poplars.

He almost turns to her then and says – something. Says it all, maybe.

But already the words he might have spoken have been overtaken, or stopped in his throat.

Courage – is that it? He lacks? Or?

She is telling him how in the years when her family were all in residence this was the room where everyone gathered. All of them, that is, who were there regularly. There were some – . But she stops. She has gone far enough. Does not know quite why she is telling him this. But it was like that sometimes – does he not agree? You felt, for some reason you could not identify, that a person you have met – and may never see again most likely – is someone you could talk to? Who is on the same wavelength? Who would understand?

In fact she has wondered – has she seen him before? Has he been in the town at some stage previously? There is something, perhaps – some familiarity?

Even as he assures her that this is the very first time he has been there, that never before has he visited the place, that he is sorry to disappoint her – even as that is happening, from the left, from the right, the ghosts materialize. Before his eyes or if not the eyes then something deeper, they accumulate there, the grandfather, the father, the mother, the wife. A Christmas, was it? He can see in the corner the tree with the candles, lit, every one, anticipating a future that is long gone by now.

He feels how the tussle in his head is then, how the moment teeters. Mastery! It is his. But under his guard and despite all the effort he sees them appear, the boy and the girl, the he and the she, as they had been then. Sixteen and fifteen.

Did he ever looked fresh-faced and eager like that?

And she – with the round cheek and chin, so unlike the one that he sees now before him?

It's no good, Anne.

The boy that he had been is speaking out with a definiteness he can hardly recognize.

It's no good, Anne. I'm going.

Do you have to? They'll worry.

I must go. I must. But you won't tell them, will you?

Would he like to see more? She is asking him now. There is plenty of space on the next two floors. Space for a family. For guests. For his friends.

Is he tempted at all? He sees in his mind's eye the room where he slept. To visit himself there? No no. Impossible.

He can sense immediately her disappointment. Not to his taste, is that it, she is saying. It is understandable. She herself is leaving in the morning. It is difficult to let things go, she has found. But finally, now, she has done so, almost. A new future, elsewhere. Freedom. She hopes so.

He hears himself saying she has misunderstood. He will take the place. Twelve months, he is telling her. He would like to take it for as long as possible.

Two little pink patches spring up on her cheeks. Joy? Or relief?

She presses the auctioneer's card in his hand and before he can realize it he is out in the street. Her pale eyed look is the last thing he sees as she closes the door on him.

Is it the same street? It seems busier now, traffic going by in both directions and the pavements awash with a throng of people.

Perhaps it is rush hour, all the commuters coming home? Or there is some rhythm animating things that he does not understand?

He feels the hard edge of the card she has given him there in his pocket. Rennie & Taylor. Auctioneers. Valuers.

He pauses outside. *Your Dream Home*, the sign says. *Make it a Reality*. In the window he sees his own reflection, smaller suddenly than he would have thought possible. From the clock on St Mary's the hour chimes out. He has only to put his hand on the latch. To say to himself, I have made the decision. I am returning.

The cars go by steadily, one after another, and behind them he can hear the thrum of the bus in the distance approaching. He sees himself on it, going away, traversing the straight, traversing the bend, with the town behind him. What he is. What he was.

A land cruiser edges slowly past him, its windows darkened.

From the auctioneer's office someone is beckoning him to come in.

He puts his hand up.

It needs some more thought, perhaps that is it. No need to rush. He can decide later.

He finds he is walking, slowly then quickly. *Posh Fish. Waitrose.* He hears the bus revving its engine already at the stop ahead of him, sees its blunt nose vibrating, sees the tyres begin their inevitable easing over the asphalt.

He is running now, running as though for his life. Running and waving.

As he stumbles forward onto the bus, the door swivels to with a sigh behind him.

A single, is it?

Yes, a single.

The bus is accelerating up the street, past *Rennie & Taylor*, past *Archie's Kebab*, and now, here it is, past *Sterret's Bakery*.

Is that a face he sees in the window? Not her face, is it?

As the town falls away and the road opens up, he settles back into the seat, which holds him. The hedges speed by in a blur that is comforting. No need to rush it. He has all the time in the world.

3. AWAY

Heritage Road

In Connecticut the air hangs heavy. In July time, nothing happens. You sit on the veranda swinging your feet and the cat comes out and stretches in the corner and then goes in again.

Northampton brewery. Sipping a long beer. The wet runs down the outside of the glass sweating with cool. Ninety-two degrees and rising. Humidity eighty-eight percent. Is this your past, or your future? You get on the telephone to Helen who sounds surprised to hear you. Fourteen years isn't as long as it might be. And then Beat comes on, sounding very much frailer than before.

Are we going to see you? Beat says, trying to keep the hope in his voice from showing.

Friday? you say.

Beat makes a sound like a little sigh that he's heaved up from somewhere.

Friday will be fine.

Driving through time in a little white car with a sporty appearance and the engine a bit like a pulse that will just go on beating.

Don't forget, I say. No sex. No talk about former husbands. No jibes about lovers.

Amy giggles, and crosses and uncrosses her legs, and puts her foot on the accelerator. The industrial strip of a small Connecticut town called Lampert goes past us. We have been together ten years on and off. Mostly it has been on, but there have been one or two off-times. At the moment she is taking her Prozac with a new regularity. Last night she turned to me and said, Maybe it's love.

We come out of the strip quite suddenly and a lake falls out before us glittering and secret. A bird that I don't know the name of comes up like a sleek sided meteor out of the water which breaks from its wings in a shower of glass.

Don't you just *love* America? she says, accentuating her drawl ever so slightly and making a funny face.

There are some things about America I'm fond of, I tell her.

She gives me a look that I can't wholly fathom.

The new world can creep up on you, she says.

Woodbury has a lot of houses with flags on that proclaim their historic value.

Gee, says Amy. That one was 1750. You don't get them much older than that.

They are clapboard and very well kept and some of them have quite grand steps all surmounted with pillars. I ask her what the pillars are made of, but she doesn't know. They look like cardboard. Maybe they put them there just for the look of it. I get out of the car and sneak up and knock on one of them. My knuckles make a solid, no-nonsense kind of a sound. The pillars are wooden. When I tell Amy she purses her lips in a surprised but neutral kind of a way.

I guess the old things had to be genuine, she says.

We park the car and look round the antique shops. We are early, and it wouldn't do to be early for Beat and Helen. Beat never liked it if I was early. He ran his life on a clock that wasn't variable. Maybe he had been different when he was younger. The way things were in our family I could never know.

This is cute, Amy says, brandishing a 1980s imitation toasting fork. I tell her she looks like a boy ready for the duello. She blushes and puts the fork away from her. There's a fan going in the corner which makes the hairs on her arm stand up.

Gonna be another hot one, says the man behind the desk.

Through the bluish haze of just-gone-lunchtime heat we go for an ice cream. She sucks up the residue of hers with relish. I leave most of mine congealing on the pressed glass saucer.

You didn't finish it, she says accusingly.

We sit on in the shop enjoying the air conditioning and the cool draught falls down around us like a shower.

Cool air! Amy says. This is lovely!

She stretches her arms high up over her head and shakes out her hair in a wave down over her shoulder. The hooter from the sawmills we passed a couple of miles back sounds off. I look at my watch.

Time we were going.

Amy lets her breath out with a *whuuf!* and puts her hands palm down on the edge of the table.

Anything you say, Ella, Amy says.

Those old things. They make you think. Ancient times. Ancient houses.

My grandmother on my mother's side had long hair and looked like a gypsy and was called Ella Marina.

Sounds a bit like a whale in a glass case. You ever see one of those?

Beat pushes his hat back and crouches down. Our heads are at the same level. I have spilled ice cream down my frock and have been crying. He wipes the snot off my top lip with his handkerchief.

No need to cry over a trifle.

He speaks in a strange way and I know he is from somewhere different.

America, he says. Know where America is? It's way over on the other side of the world.

His mouth goes from one side of his face to the other and I know he is smiling.

My name is Beat. I knew your Daddy when he was a young thing.

At that a bubble comes up that is like a hiccough and I start crying.

He puts his arm around me and scoops me with him into the upright.

It's OK sweetheart. Beat will look after you, he says.

My father was a very old man when he had me. His brother, Beat's father, was fifteen years older.

Your father was a fine man, Beat said. We were like brothers.

He lifted his shoulders expressively when he said the word.

Uncle Lew had gone out long ago to begin a new life and had married three times. Beat and his stepmother didn't get on. Once she'd put Beat out in the street in Manhattan. I don't know how old he was, seven maybe, eight at the most. I would think of him stepping out into the street with a fistful of tight little fingers clutching his suitcase and the vertical strips of the skyline wavy with tears.

When the accident happened and my parents got killed, Beat came over. He sweet talked the lawyers to get rid of the stuffy old house with a clock that ticked on and an Aunt as duenna. There was an owl perched very stiff on a papier mâché branch that I waved goodbye to. It had dust on the scales of its feet and a layer of dust like a film on the cusp of its eye.

There are parts of Connecticut that are more like the South, everyone says so. The swamp and the bayou and the hot heavy air that comes on, and the evening.

That was where he took me first, down to Louisiana. His hat on the back of his head. We jumped off the train while it was still moving. Ready, steady! he said. And we jumped.

I had a little frock with cherry sprigs on. We got off the train and the soft thing of the nearly tropic touched the flesh of my legs. A big bright bird with red on its wings went up from a branch and we watched it.

Cockatoo, Beat said knowledgeably, pushing his hat to the very back of his head.

He went and he came back again. He left me with white people and brown people and yellow people and people whose skin was black and glistening.

The world in all its richness, he said.

What he did, or didn't do, I didn't know then and never found out later.

We got off in San Diego. The bells on the crossing went *ding ding ding!* as the train snaked off, ever so slowly, all through the mile of its length or more, and slid past the sea-baked air on its way down south.

Down south was where the world was. Beat told me about the Inca cities rising right up in their blocks into the sky. He told me of greed, and gold, and *conquistadors*. He told me of beautiful women with jewellery adorning their necks and their wrists and their fingers.

Love, he said, Power. You get taken over.

I was older by that time, and sat up beside him and looked through the window of the train.

And Beat made a lot of money, doing whatever it was Beat did.

The hats that he wore on the back of his head got sleeker. There was a patina that he seemed to acquire on the fabric of his suits. He stood in front of the mirror one day and said, This is what wealth looks like.

I liked what wealth looked like. I took his hand and we went out together into an air that was strangely colder, New York, October, leaves crinkling up at the edges in Central Park and falling, falling, racing on the wind all the way down Fifth Avenue, topsy, turvey, this way, that way, but always the same direction, like there was somewhere very particular to go.

Back home at last. Damp and misty. The English air is cold, the touch of it strange. I am wearing a gingham school dress when he comes, too late by far, to erect the monument.

Did they do it like I said?

I think so.

We stand in front of it shivering. It is bitter June. My dress is tight at the chest and I see him look, and then quickly look away.

He holds the umbrella up for both of us. The rain drips off the spokes and falls down round us in a circle.

The monument is square and simple. I told him I wanted a great big angel holding a scroll.

Angels are old-fashioned, he wrote to me. Why not have a griffin in either corner? The griffin is a magical bird.

And so, two griffins pulling at some unspecified space, and between them, two names.

Him I can remember vaguely, a scent, a quirk of movement, or a shade come up occasionally with the utmost clarity. Of her there is no remnant, not quite true, the ruby pattern of an evening party dress.

Did you know her? I ask him.

No, he says. I never met her in my life.

And then he does an odd thing, crosses himself, and for a moment I could think that he was crying, but conclude after a short consideration that it is just the rain.

He holds the umbrella up for both of us.

Behind the shutter in the car which keeps the driver off he takes my hand.

You happy? he says.

Nope, I say.

He holds my hand a little tighter. He is staying in a smart hotel in Mayfair. We drive back to London with the windscreen wipers going at high speed.

What then? Love?

I build it, I speak it. It comes like blocks on my tongue. It is constructed like a set of ancient edifices, one mass then another. A thing interlinking. The city of gold on the far mountain. And into its old rites I gradually initiate myself.

That year. The one after.

He writes and tells me he has found a woman that he wants as wife, and can he. I write back, I am very grown up after all, and say he may.

I send him an Audubon print of a red cockatoo that I found in a book. It is perched on a branch and the sun bats up off of its feathers and hits out right into your eye.

Some bird, he writes back. I'll think of you each time I look, and the thought will be treasure.

And then in deep country, with the mist lifting and coming down.

Plenty of mountains. No gold cities. It rained, more than it did anything else, and though there were a lot of birds none of them, except in the Autumn sometimes when the sun flashed off a well-oiled wing-tip, none of them had much colour.

His wife, who was good to him, took ill one summer and suddenly died.

Then there was a long gap, and he was in the land of the Incas, and I had cards occasionally.

Amy changes gear with a little discordant sound. She is pouting. You know from long usage that you had better hold her hand. It is a small hand, not entirely formed you would think, like a child's.

Not long, I say.

We are driving through the woods again, very dense and secret. The frontier as it was comes up out of them and then recedes.

It will soon be over.

And then to distract her I explain that Helen is his third wife, there was one down south that I never heard much of. When he let me know he was marrying Helen I flew out.

The engine has dropped to a purr. The trees going past us. Very neat. Very English. A wood with deep shadows goes off over to our right.

And what did you think? She slows down as she asks me.

We won't be long now.

The sign tells us *Heritage Road*. The houses give way to a flat open land.

And I say, I don't know. But Helen's all right.

And no babies?

No babies.

The house on our right up a drive with no flag. The white boards, so cool, overlap in the heat. To the back is a lake with a little boat moored, and the water like skin with a rise and a fall sets it bobbing.

Helen comes out, and then Beat, with a stick.

And his hair that was black going back with a sleek, turned to grey.

He straightens up. His eyes are a little rheumy. His mouth still from side to side on his face but a little less certain.

You look the same, Beat.

You too, Ella.

To see the both of you together! Helen says.

A very civilised afternoon. Little napkins to put on your knee. Cranberry juice. Cocktails. And Helen brings the photographs, she bears them up in her two arms like they were precious. And those old times flood up, and I can feel them rise about my chest and throat.

Helen is very dapper, with little spots of gold at her earlobes and a bright red kerchief circling her neck.

Oh yes, oh yes, she says, this one! This one, when Beat went over. Fifty-seven? Fifty-six?

Your father? says Amy.

He stands very straight, with his hand gripping Beat's shoulder, looking ridiculously young.

And where was it taken? Helen says. Of course you don't know. It was way before you came along.

Just a year, Beat offers.

Amy is giving him one of her analysing looks.

And this one, Helen says, is rare, but oh! she was pretty, oh my, so she was – !

Your mother, Beat says.

And there is her face that I suddenly know I remember, and the ruby red dress without colour, and the scent of her hair.

And she is with Beat who looks down at her fondly, and she looks up into his eyes.

Helen has got out her camera.

I'll take one of you, Amy offers, very bright, very gay, all of a sudden. Let's capture that family resemblance!

There's a *click!* and I blink as the flash dissolves back in the little red dot. Amy is looking from one to the other.

A gift for posterity, she says.

And when I turn she has gone off with Helen, her heels clacking on the paving, her laughter up somewhere underneath the trees.

Your friend, he says.

Yes, I say.

You didn't marry.

And then they are out on the lake, she and Helen. The little red splash and the tinkle of laughter. And who is it wielding the oars I don't know. But the boat surges forward with the prow of it cutting the skin of the lake like the edge of a knife.

The afternoon sun has turned them to cut-out.

There are pigeons coo-cooing up in the trees, too early.

Remember – ? He says, and the smell of the south comes up out of the water and hits us, and the shriek of a bird comes up with it from out of the trees, much too high and too raucous.

And he lifts up his head as he hears it and he turns, and the wet on the front of my dress from my eyes that I can't stop from falling drops down with no sound.

And he puts his arm around me and scoops me up to him.

His breath is like glass on my cheek as he breathes it.

It's OK sweetheart. Beat will look after you, he says.

THIRUVEGA

They had landed in Mumbai on 25th February. It was just coming in to the hotter season but they did not let that put them off.

They were due for their appointment, in the Bandra district, well away from the centre, at eleven thirty. The driver at first had difficulty in finding it. When he squinted at the address and said, Is it medical? she had nodded. We will find it, he said, looking at her from under his eyelashes. We will find it for sure.

There was a reception desk with a queue already and beyond that was a tiny waiting room. At first they were the only Europeans. The receptionist smiled and took their details, just her name and the time of the appointment, then they took their shoes off and went and sat down in the straight-backed waiting-room chairs.

The consultant, Dr Mrs Kandesh Aliyah, was friendly. I think she liked us, William said afterwards. There was a fifty percent chance of success which sounded small but seemed enormous. One chance in two. The coin falling this way or that way. When Dr Mrs Kandesh Aliyah said, Yes, of course, I am sure we can help you, she had felt something she could not at first identify. It was a small, warm kernel of immediate feeling. She searched around for something to call it but could come up with no adequate name.

They had both dressed carefully for the appointment and looked what they were. William's cropped white hair and soft skin were evidence of his prosperity. Her own designer linen moved with her easily. She had a haircut which emphasized the youthful line of her cheekbones. Dr Mrs Kandesh Aliyah had appraised her.

Fifty-one, yes indeed, Dr Mrs Kandesh Aliyah said, and wrote on her paper. She knew what she was now. Dr Mrs Kandesh Aliyah would provide both host and donor. They hand the baby over as soon as it is born, in the hospital. Her name and William's name would be on the birth certificate. We will choose a light-skinned donor, Dr Mrs Kandesh Aliyah had said to her. You will find that people will say how much the child is like you. It is living together. These things are a matter of science. But they are also a matter of the heart.

The flight to Calicut seemed inordinately long. William talked excitedly at first about the baby. But then he had fallen into a sleep and she noticed the two bright spots that settled on his cheekbones, then the pallor, a peculiar, papery look spreading out around his eyes.

In Arrivals she handled the luggage herself, pushing the trolley through the automatic doors with William behind her. Rajesh and the driver were waiting. They are here, William, she said, It will be alright now. It was only afterwards that she realized he had not replied.

The road which zigzagged through the paddy fields narrowed and eventually gave out altogether.

Here now, Rajesh said. Thiruvega. Welcome.

And she had seen the house with its gables and overhangs, and the marble hall with its archways reflected, and Amini and Sahita Banda were bobbing and bowing, and the chef, who was called Simon, stepped forward and handed them posies. William stumbled as he accepted his and a flower, bougainvillea she thought it was, very red and papery, came away and dropped onto the marble. It did not matter and the moment passed off successfully. William did not stumble again, not even when they were going up the stairs.

By the fourth day they had settled into a routine. William had the best bedroom with a high ceiling and windows that looked out over the pool and garden. Her own room was on the interior, with a wooden ceiling and low, louvered windows. Across the drive was a coconut grove with Rajesh's house on the far side of it. He and his wife lived with their son there, and another baby due, any hour, any minute. They were waiting. They were expecting. But nevertheless, he had said she could call him at any time in the night if there was need to. His number was on a pad by the telephone. He had shown it to her and she repeated the number, seven five eight two one.

She climbed up the spiral stairs to the Paddy Pura every morning to write her journal and then joined William for breakfast. He was up to his one-and-a-half kilometre swim, in two lots admittedly. She saw emerging from the flesh around his middle a latent musculature. Their life together was, she believed, similarly emerging. William spoke about how it would be when the little one was with them.

Life, he said. Life! D'you see? This place is teeming with it.

He reached out and took hold of her forearm, gripping it tightly. What she remembered most afterwards was the sound of sweeping, Amini and Sahita Banda wielding their brooms with their backs bent over, sweeping and sweeping throughout the best part of the day.

They had been there a week. It was almost dark and a thunderstorm was approaching. You could see it on the hills, particularly to the south, and it vied with the fireworks that erupted at regular intervals from the nearby temple. A wind came up too and the chanting from the temple rose and fell with it. Up above, the sky was relatively clear still, and behind the palm fronds you could see an intermittent moon.

The references had come that day, out of the ether onto William's BlackBerry. I *been with Dr Mrs & now waiting my son who come in July.* That was from Caracas. *We have our child,* wrote Mrs B from Godalming. *Our lives are complete now.* Something about these messages made her want to cry.

You've got to hand it to them, William had said. They're overtaking us. It's a new world we're in, and we can't get away from it.

Simon had cooked a special Tandoor dinner, and they watched admiringly as he reached down into the red-hot chimney and flicked the chapattis onto the curving side-part just above the flame.

Very special skill, Simon said. Bad burn to the hand here is possible.

The lights went out during the main course. Simon laughed in the darkness and she could see his teeth as he stepped forward to flick the emergency switch.

She persuaded William to go and sit with her out on the veranda. Through the arches you could look out over the pool and see how the palm trees were already leaning over, and hear how the wind was gathering in the hollow where the tank was, and see the moon coming and going, yellow, white, pink, orange, through the banks of cloud.

Eventually the wind broke everything open and the rain pelted in sideways. She waited for each flash and explosion and heard herself laughing. The shutters on the roof were banging and Rajesh and Simon were running from one end of the house to the other, battening the doors. When she was soaked to the skin and William almost, she had said, I suppose we should go in. And William, lifting his shirt away from his shoulders, had smiled and said, The papers. We should sign them. When we go up, eh? We should sign them tonight.

On the way upstairs she had to steady his arm just once on the first landing. She went to her room and got the papers and a pen but by the time she went in to William he was already in bed with the covers pulled up around him, and his eyes were closed.

Tap-tap-tap it went. Tap-tap-tap. Perhaps it was the rain dripping into the bucket on the landing. She unlocked the door to the outside gallery and went downstairs very quietly, in her nightdress, barefoot. She knew where the key was and put the heavy metal in the lock and turned it smoothly. She lifted the chocks that kept the door barred and stepped outside.

The moon looked thin and slightly acidic on the paving. Her shadow wobbled beside her at a backward angle. Something rustled in the coconut grove and she wondered briefly if it might not be a snake. At the end of the garden the paddy fields looked oddly bald and available. She stopped in the arch of the Paddy Pura and put her hand on the gate.

Madam. Madam! It was like a little hiss, the wind under the mango leaves, a dry leaf sliding along the veranda wall.

Madam. Madam!

A patch of white and then it was gone.

She pressed back into the shelter of the Paddy Pura and steadied her breathing. Even and quiet, that was how she wanted it.

He came very slowly down the path, his fingers splayed and his head tilted. She watched him covering the ground between them very steadily and purposefully. When he was about ten feet away and she was sure he must have seen her, he stopped.

It is all right, Madam, it will be all right.

He held his hand out.

Very special flower that good to make babies. There is no name for it, but it grow always next to the Tree of Life.

Behind him the house looked dark and closed in on itself. By the tank there was a rustle, then the plop of something unidentifiable dropping in.

Madam?

A door slammed and a small, thin cry set up in the distance, like the teasing of a mechanical saw.

Rajesh was calling. Simon. Simon!

She stepped out from under the Paddy Pura and found she was alone.

Now it was almost light, or was it the moon? She let herself back into the house and climbed quickly to the landing. A bird had shrieked outside the window. Wah-ha-ha-ha. Wah-ha-ha-ha. She heard it again, or really heard it. A high-pitched bubbling that was half way between a gurgle and a scream.

She ran into William's room, her white nightdress billowing around her. It was not light but half light, grey and pale buff, the edges of everything were indeterminate. She made out his profile, head thrown back, mouth open.

He was sweating and as she tried to take hold of his arm to lift him the flesh was slippery and he slid down out of her hands.

She gave up and ran out of the room and down the stairs, shouting for Rajesh, calling for Simon. Then she was outside and it was light now, the shape of things was emerging fully, and behind the paddy fields the sky had begun to glow.

They came running, Rajesh with his dhoti tucked up at the waist and his sandals flapping. Simon in his cut-offs, pushing his chest out as he ran.

A small mishap, that was what it was, in their respectful opinion. They came to find her on the veranda just before lunch. The smell of cooked spice drifted across from the kitchen. Sir was resting, and seemed quite recovered. It was the heat no doubt, or he had eaten something, a small aberration.

Rajesh invited her over to see his new baby, his and his dear wife's, arrived in a rush just last night, in the early hours.

A fine little girl, he said then, puffing out his shoulders.

She looked like her mother. But light skinned, very light skinned indeed, which was surprising.

The child was in an earth-coloured cloth, looking shrivelled and ancient. You will hold her, Rajesh said. Each visitor coming to see is a gift and a blessing. She will grow up tall and forward, Inshallah. She will lead a good life.

She expected a weight but there was almost none, the child in the earth-coloured cloth could have been a phantom. Then it moved slightly, it was alive and sentient. Through the folds of cloth the warmth of it seeped into her hands and she saw how the blood was beating in a blue vein just above the eyebrow. It was almost transparent and she saw the shape of its bones, the spread of its skeleton.

Fine baby, eh? Simon said.

He was holding his hands behind his back and grinning at her.

Fine baby, she said.

When William came down it was almost as normal. He did not swim, but he would do so tomorrow. There were peacocks, five of them, that came to the tank to drink, it was a good omen.

She went upstairs and brought down the papers, thinking that now at last they would sign them, but William was asleep, his head tilted back and his white hair awry on the blue cushion. From the kitchen, Amini's voice bubbled up, high and then quiet again. She heard Simon cry out, brusque, slightly peevish, and Rajesh's quick intercession bringing the argument to an end.

She smoothed William's hair back on his forehead and he mumbled something. *Life!* he had said. *This place is teeming with it.*

She folded the papers and put them away. A door banged, and the deep heat of the afternoon settled around her. It was quiet now, very quiet.

From Rajesh's house the child cried once and briefly. Then nothing. She watched for a minute a speck of down like a dandelion clock, rising and falling, rising and falling, there on the edge of William's top lip.

Rue des Etrangers

The oranges on the corner of the market stall were as luscious when she passed them at twelve noon as they had been first thing in the morning. She noticed particularly the smoothness, the firmness, making you want to run your hands over them. Not that she did that. Not even after all these years of being here. To pick up the produce and feel it in your fingers, to pressure and test, and put it back again – so very European. She could not get used to it. It was not the only thing she had been unable to get used to. That was why, perhaps, she still felt an outsider. Felt so increasingly as the seasons turned over, and the hues of the fruit and the vegetables she walked past every morning changed from brown to yellow to green to russet. She was lucky to be privy to such abundance, to such beauty. If only she could take that luck and transform it into – what? Happiness? She remembered the feeling. A warmth, was it? A certain lusciousness, there at the very heart and centre of herself.

She wondered, as she turned the corner away from Avenue Niel, whether Madame Ferrand would be troublesome this morning. She wondered that every morning. And for most mornings recently, Madame Ferrand had, indeed, proved to be troublesome. It was age – was it? Or merely becoming the thing that you were – even more so? Madame Ferrand had always been troublesome. It was what she was paid for – to deal with that trouble, to handle it, to savour it, to constrain and console. It was her raison d'être and had been for these past ten years of her grown up life.

Ten years! The traffic on Rue des Etrangers, thick now, thicker than she had been used to, seemed to mock her. It was going somewhere. All these people, with their things to do, their lives to lead, their hopes and fears to fulfil or ameliorate. The stood at the small lights by Allée du Chemin, waiting to cross. What was she? Nothing but a small speck, backwards and forwards, forwards and backwards, daily, weekly.

The scent of a lunch underway wafted out from a kitchen as she crossed the grating that marked the passageway. Cité Berryer. She had used to come there in her best frock and those shoes with their little, spindly heels. For lunch. For dinner. They had come there together, she and Antoine, in those years when the future had seemed like a gift.

Did it seem like a threat now? That same future? There was less of it? Antoine was a memory, and not one she visited very often. He came to her sometimes, through dream, not through memory. Came to her, life size – bigger than life size, as he always had been. My dear Anna, he said, there in the dream, holding his hand out. In dream as in life, always about to say something. Ten years. He would be middle aged now – more than middle aged. No doubt his smile and the way he avoided eye contact at particular moments would have stayed with him.

The frock and the shoes and Antoine with his hand out. She had time, she would make time. She turned into Cité Berryer with caution, for the cobbles were greasy with last night's rain. There it was, at the end, *Le Snooty Fox*. The awning looked very turn of the century – nineties, even. The paintwork, a medium chocolate brown – had that once been fashionable? The menu too – du foie de veau grillé, Carpaccio de Thon.

She stood close up to the window, as close as she could, pretending to scrutinize the menu. There was the interior, looking just the same. Pristine table cloths. An air of seclusion, a promise of intimacy. At the table on the far right she saw a young couple – not that young actually. Well heeled. Relaxed. The woman was removing the skin of an orange with the aid of a knife, nimbly, assuredly, the ribbon of peel easing away in a complete corkscrew. Her look of extreme concentration gave way to a smile of pure joy. They leaned into one another across the table, the woman was laughing and holding out the orange to the man, who smiled and took it. They looked as though they were both absolutely sure of something. Some truth. Some secret.

Madame? Vous désirez?

No no, she would not be lunching today, thank you. Thank you.

There was no help. There was nothing she needed. She turned and went back too hastily across the cobbles, with the waiter watching her.

The stairway to Madame Ferrand's apartment seemed steeper than usual. She never used the lift, preferring instead to take the exercise.

She could see immediately that Madame Ferrand was not in a mood that would make her life easy.

Maman is a little down today, the daughter said.

Was there a reason? Could she do anything?

It is just the usual. Do what you can. If anyone can jolly Maman along, it is you, Anna, surely.

The wheelchair was difficult to manoeuvre out of the mouth of the lift, and out of the front door to the apartments, equally. She maintained a light flow of conversation throughout these undertakings. Once they were out in the street, silence fell between them. The silence was all right, as long as all the other sounds were around them. The thrum of the traffic. The snatches of conversation they heard from the people who passed them. The wail of a siren from a few streets away, the Gendarmerie, or an ambulance maybe.

They were going to the park, that much had been established. The Parc Monceau. It was only a relatively small space, but it generally exercised a soothing effect. The trees. The children. It was not until she had stationed the wheelchair next to a bench and got out the sandwiches that Madame Ferrand confessed she was not feeling so good today. In her head. In her heart. It was not physical.

If it was not physical, then what was it?

Tristesse, merely. Did Anna not understand tristesse? Did no one in the world understand it, except her? If Monsieur Ferrand had not gone and died! If her daughter were fonder!

The sandwiches remained untouched in her lap, on the blanket that swathed her knees today as it did every day.

Those hands in the lap, folding and unfolding. How old they were! Older than you'd almost think possible.

Madame Ferrand was recounting now, as she did most days, the past in its glory. How happy they had been, she and Monsieur. And how companionable. Closer than two peas in a pod, if it was allowable to put it that way.

And of course it was true that today of all days this would be on her mind, this relationship, this closeness. For tomorrow was the date of their wedding anniversary. All those years ago. They were young. They were healthy. And the world itself – that had a youth to it.

Tomorrow would have been their fiftieth anniversary. Half a century gone! Where did it go to? And instead of celebration, there she would be, the same as always, the light, the shade, the day quite interminable.

Would it have been possible, Anna wondered afterwards, to have let the flow of those observations wash over her as she had done so often, as she had to, in order to survive each day, to go back to her own place and have her supper with a degree of equilibrium, and watch a little programme on the television, and retire to her own bed, narrower than it had been, with some hope of sleeping?

For she saw, did she not, in Madame Ferrand, herself in the future, but without the memories? Without even that kernel of warmth to keep her querulous and seeking?

She found herself asking what they had done, on those days of anniversary celebration. A party, perhaps? A family gathering?

Madame's hands now were clasped in an animation that would have been surprising had you not seen that her eyes, too, were lit up with something that was quite unlike what usually resided there.

A party – no. Yes! A gathering of sorts. A dinner. A lunch. Monsieur Ferrand had been wonderful with lunches. Exquisite food. The finest wines. And always, for pudding, her favourite for which he knew she had a considerable weakness. *Rosace à l'orange.* It was not something you saw or even heard about these days. But how she had loved it. And how they had shared it, he and she, with each other, with their friends.

Madame Ferrand continued talking happily enough about the lunches, the menus, the conviviality, all the way home, so that even her daughter was moved to comment that the afternoon outing had done her good.

Only you know how to look after Maman, she said then to Anna. To tell you the truth, we are thinking of moving her out to a home. She does not want to. But what can we do, if things continue to go, as they seem to, from bad to worse?

Perhaps it was on the way back through the streets that the idea took root. The streets with their people and the lights coming on as the darkness took hold, and the sense of an energy drawn up for some purpose – what was it? Just living?

Perhaps it was as she went up the stairs and let herself into her small apartment, finding it exactly the same as she had left it?

She put on the overhead light and got out her old laptop. She did not use it very often these days. But now she looked up the recipe on Google. *Rosace à l'orange*. The image of a half globe of rich-looking sponge topped by glistening circlets of orange leapt up before her. Preparation time two hours. Cooking time two hours. *A genoise sponge base is soaked in Grand Marnier and topped with oodles of rich custard and candied orange slices.*

Could she – ? Would it – ?

Serves ten was the warning below the ingredients. Ten people. She did not know anyone at all. Had not, for a long time.

It would be no good. It was impossible to contemplate. A lunch – the idea! When had she last held one?

It was getting quite late by the time she had eaten her cheese omelette. She generally had a cheese omelette at night, or maybe with prawns. It was quick, and the size of the pan she used meant she did not have to cook more than was necessary for one person.

She lay down to sleep. It was not easy. *Monsieur Ferrand was wonderful with lunches.* And the edible glaze of the oranges there on the half globe of sponge. *Using a mandoline or a very sharp knife, slice the oranges thinly.*

She woke up with the decision quite fully made, she did not know how, and spent the morning executing her intention.

She collected Madame Ferrand at twelve thirty, as they had arranged, and told her they were going a different route today.

The old woman was silent. Adrift in her thoughts? At one with her memories?

It was a long way to push, over the uneven slabs of the street. She expected protest, but none was forthcoming. Madame Ferrand seemed quite somnambulant.

She only asked once, not even querulously, Are we nearly there yet? But quite oddly, and quite out of character, she appeared to be enjoying the ride.

It was a squash in the lift, which was not meant for two, and certainly not meant to accommodate a wheelchair.

As they approached the top, the very sixth floor where the apartment was, a sweetish aroma sifted in through the air vent.

Madame Ferrand sat up, in as much as she could, and said, What? And What!

If a heart can be said to be beating so fast that it is in danger of overtaking itself, so Anna's heart was beating at that moment.

It was as if she had run for a very long way. Would anyone come? Would the – ? Could she – ?

She unlocked the door and pushed the chair in and the room looked as good as she had hoped it might do.

The table in the centre was set with a white cloth. There were the cheeses, rich and redolent. There was the cut bread, crispy and fresh, and a clean towel over it.

She whisked the towel away and stationed Madame Ferrand at the head, presiding.

While Madame asked her questions which she tried not to answer, who, what and why, she got out the wine, uncorking the white and decanting the red, listening all the while for a step on the stair or the sound of the lift.

Is it just us two?

Madame Ferrand looked slightly less buoyed than she had done initially.

The clock struck the three quarter.

Perhaps we had better – .

There was a sound at the door – a knock, was it?

When she opened it she saw the quiet little chemist from two floors down, who she had spoken to once about a matter of garbage.

As she ushered him in, the lift creaked to a stop and the metal door opened with a hiss and a clink. The girl student from below who annoyed her at night by playing the violin past ten thirty was coming towards her with a bunch of flowers held tight in her hand.

Then the old Commander, who lived at the back, came puffing out at the next exhalation.

That was it, the five of them.

There they were, together around the table.

They were talking. Engaging. And who then – ? And what if – ?

It was energy, impetus. Somebody laughed – it was life, wasn't it?

She brought out the cake with a flourish and noticed the oranges on it had wilted somewhat. That did not matter. There were oohs and aahs, and in a moment, the five spoons were being wielded.

What did it taste like? She could never have said, exactly, after.

They raised their glasses.

To Madame Ferrand, and to Monsieur also, wherever he may be.

There were three cheers, and the glasses clinked in unison.

To dear Anna, Madame Ferrand said then, who has always looked after me.

To Anna, they said, and raised their glasses.

She was late getting Madame Ferrand back home. The daughter was testy.

As she turned to go, Madame Ferrand put out her hand.

Come dear. Kiss me.

That papery cheek, with its own special warmth, quite unexpected.

Same time tomorrow.

Same time. Don't forget!

Madame Ferrand was smiling, still smiling, as the door closed behind her, and she stepped out into the street.

4. NOWHERE

THE LITTLE LOST ONES

They drove up the coast from Malmö through Göteborg and north towards the border. They were in a car that was two years old, they were playing Sibelius and she in particular was watching the forest as they drove through it. The individual trees were extremely tall and straight and of a dark green colour that seemed to have a certain blue to it. They had recently lost a baby and both were grieving. They looked through their separate expanses of car window at the intense whiteness of the sky.

It was not as though this was the first baby they had lost, there had been several. Small scraps of something that turned out to be nothing, that was how she thought of it. As well as the grief there was a very unsettling sense of having been cheated. Somebody, somewhere, had done them out of what they were entitled to. It was not fair, she had cried out, looking very red and ugly soon after it had happened. He saw the dark interior of her nostrils and was repelled by it. The sight of it rendered the process of breathing intolerable. Even the sound, the air coming in and going out again, was more than he could bear.

They had been planning this trip a long time, even before the baby (it had been a boy) was thought of. They had not been thinking of children for some time now. He told her they should focus on something else, and they had deliberately done so. The effort made his eyes bloodshot. He appeared to have hunched his whole self around a core of some adamantine material. She on the other hand seemed like a paper cut-out that has been blown away.

This road, he said, perhaps to break the silence that was in his head more than the silence that was between them. It lay out ahead of them in a twist between the pine trees. The edges appeared crenelated. It was like it was not a road but a fabric thing that someone had laid there. It unrolled in front of the wheels of the car through the dips and rises. They both felt at the same instant that it was not a road, that they were not really driving. Even the pine trees were a back-cloth that had been painted. Living itself, the flesh and the blood of it, was a fake.

They had not all been boys, there were four of them, the little lost ones, two of each sex although one had been so early as to be indeterminate. Still, she had known it was a girl, you knew these things. It was the second and she had gone into it very hopeful. She had known as soon as her husband came and cried out that from this encounter she was destined to get pregnant. At that time she had a positive relation with destiny. But as the number of little ones lost seemed to be increasing she wondered whether she might not have offended someone. Which god after all would look down and decree the moment of severance? She was not a fatalist exactly, but as the losses accrued she felt that there was a force of something out there against her in the world.

He drove with his hands clasping the wheel very tightly. He was conscious of his wife sitting still and straight beside him, staring at the road. The Sibelius, which he loved, was coming to an end, *Karelia*, and next she would put on the violin concerto. He did not know whether he could stand that, the rising and falling and the drawn-out diminuendos. The forest around him however, that appeared to be endless, told him he could stand it. He was consoled by the fact that there was no other traffic on the road.

Shall we stop? he said. His wife yawned and stretched and he thought how odd it was to see a natural movement. The trip was a good idea and through it they could put the rest behind them. He imaged the little side streets of Oslo, the glass-fronted cafés, the cobbles in front of the Amundsen museum. They would walk along by the water and agree how very grey and endless the sea was. All the way to the North Pole he would say to her. She would look at him and really see him and, when she had considered it for a minute, she would take his hand.

He pulled off on a wide swathe of turf behind the trees. From this position the road was not visible.

Is this a good place? he said. He thought she must be hungry. It was several hours since they had last eaten anything and his hand shook a little as he pulled on the handbrake.

He saw that her face looked slightly bloated around the eye area, and how she put her hands up and down, up and down to her throat where the skin was mottled

No place is a good place, was what her look said to him. There is no such thing as a good place on this earth.

They sat without saying anything and listened to the sound of the car engine creaking. Eventually she said she was going to walk a little. Her legs were stiff from all the hours of sitting. This route up from Malmö was longer than you would have thought.

He watched her walk away, a small, beige figure among the green, and then she was quickly out of sight. Suddenly everything came into focus, the forest, the car, the silence, the minutes following one another with extreme regularity. He got out and walked around but always keeping the car in sight, you could see it from quite a distance, a splash of red that was oddly fragmentary between the trees. They had chosen the car in a moment of optimism during the last-but-one pregnancy. She had patted her stomach and smiled and made a measuring sign for the baby seat. He remembered quite distinctly the feeling that had come to him, a feeling of fullness. He had understood in that instant, briefly, how very good it was to be alive.

The husband had, if the truth be told, not wanted to try the last time. He could tell she was timing the sex again and so he was reluctant. But when she came to him in the night with eager hands and smelling of soap he could not resist her. Afterwards when she lay back and he saw the flutter of her eyelids he felt estranged.

They had bought baby clothes the first time and had them in a small, brown bag up in the attic. Two weeks ago before the trip he had come home and found her crying over them. The tiny, white jacket with its satin ribbons looked bereft.

If he wanted a child at all (and sometimes, he acknowledged in his most secret self, he doubted it) then it was to do with extending out into the future. In our children we are immortal. He thought he had read that somewhere but could not be sure. He pictured his wife, younger and more radiant, bending over the crib in the bedroom, taking the small scrap of fleshly presence into her hands.

He imagined how it would be witnessing the child's first steps with his own heart beating and his arms tensed in by his sides, waiting to steady it. He would take the child to school and on that first day he would watch how the small shoulders under the dark blue raincoat squared themselves and moved away. He thought about this now as he waited for his wife with a growing sense of unease that bordered on irritation. It was like her to keep him waiting. She was careless. For all he knew it was something in the very structure of what she was that made her lose the children. Something that meant you could never take hold of life no matter how you wanted to. They would arrive in Oslo too late to do the things they had been planning. He saw the evening ebbing away and the white sky with the light leaching out of it. Not that it ever got really dark here, not at this time of year. But the way you could see, and what you were capable of seeing, would be subtly mutated.

The car was like a barometer in the changing light, at first seeming larger and redder but then sinking back into a uniformity. He did not want to leave the car but thought increasingly that he should go in search of her.

He tied a fleece round his waist and was soon glad of the added protection it offered him. He remembered that his wife had taken nothing with her to augment the quite meagre covering of her linen shirt. It was darker in among the trees then he had expected. He could see the twelve phosphorescent blips of his wristwatch. He had given up all thought of arriving in Oslo. He put a whistle to his lips and blew it every so often. On two occasions when the trees thinned out approximating a clearing he called her name. He thought at first that an immediate answer had come back to him. But it was his voice only, faced back to him on an echo, briefer and narrower in range than his own voice, a brusque curtailment that sounded like a mockery.

She did not know how far she had come. The light had changed, she thought it must be about four thirty. She felt around for her watch but remembered she had left it in the car on top of the dashboard. She saw it there with its single silver hand moving imperceptibly forwards on a black background. Round and round and round the face of the thing the hand would go.

She had not meant to come so far but had heard water running and been intrigued by it. It was hard to say what direction the sound came from. When she turned her head it seemed to come from ahead and from behind her. She stopped in a clearing and thought she could hear it faintly. But then there was nothing and she wondered if she had heard it at all.

What she did hear now quite clearly was the sound of voices. She saw a splash of red and thought of the car, but this red leapt and moved as she approached it and was almost immediately out of sight again.

Three of them were sitting in a circle, two were standing, it was a tableau. The parents were quite young, at least on the underside of forty, and the children ranged from about thirteen down to six. They were smooth and brown as if they lived outside and did not belong to any interior. The woman had very light hair, like white straw, tied back in a pony tail.

They were sitting by a stream, presumably the one she had heard, and the little girl was up to her ankles laughing and shivering in a swimsuit, with her arms wrapped tightly around her chest. They reminded her of an advertisement for something. Perhaps it was soap powder, or dream filling that came out of a can in a froth when you pressed the nozzle down. There was smoke coming from a small fire to the side and the hot smell of cooking came across to her. She shrank a little inside herself but it was all right, the man was gesturing and calling her over. His voice was a throaty baritone with an odd edge of lisp.

Lars, the man said, stepping forward, and Helle. Mimi and Olaf. The little one in the swimsuit waved and smiled at her from the water but apparently had no name. They began talking straight away, asking where she had come from. Would she join them for something to eat? Fish they had caught earlier. There was a small lake so full of fish you would hardly believe it, only half a mile away.

They were from Oslo, they had come South, he was a motor manufacturer, she an administrator for the hydro-electric. The children were in school and now it was the Summer holidays, their time together to enjoy one another as a family. Helle looked around her, tossing a strand of white hair back from her forehead.

It is a great treat for us, she said, to come down here together. Usually everything is in a rush, we have no time to feel we are really together. But now –. She gestured. It is different. I feel like – I feel like – . Ah, I cannot remember the word in English. In German it would be *mittelpunkt*.

The fish were fried in the pan and they handed her a plump and juicy one with the gills split open. The head was still on and the eye stared unseeingly outwards. A trickle of pink fluid ran over the lip and spread in a pool on the plate with the other juices. Here, the little girl said, she had dried herself and was standing now quite close to the woman's shoulder. Let me help you. And she scooped the head off with a deft movement and flicked it into the fire where it spat and burned.

And your own children, Helle said between mouthfuls. They are grown up now?

She replied that she had four children, and added that she had joined her husband on a business trip, and they were about to take a short break in Oslo. The children were being looked after back in London. She missed them. But it was good to get away for a bit, to be your own person. As to her children's ages: she put her knife down on the grass and made a show of counting. The eldest was eleven and the youngest was three and there was two years almost to the day between them. Yes, she said, encountering the bright looks of her interlocutors. She and her husband had been lucky. They had managed to achieve the perfect balance of two boys and two girls.

The food was settling heavily into her stomach. A slight chill had come into the air, you could feel it between the warmer currents. Helle, fixing her hair back with scaly fingers, remarked that it was like being underwater. The sun indeed had a watery tint that indicated late afternoon.

She told them she should really be getting back to her husband. He would be starting to worry about her and they still had a long way to go.

Was she sure that she knew the way? they enquired of her. The paths back through the forest could be deceptive. If she wished, they would accompany her and show her a shortcut back to the road.

But there was no need for that. She had made a mental note of each turn and was a sure of the way back as anyone could be. She had only to keep the sun behind her, a little over her left shoulder, and take the direction her shadow pointed, and she would find the way.

They saw her off with what seemed like genuine regret and the little girl kept on waving until the last moment. They were out of sight round the bend in less than a minute. Now she was quite alone and the trees appeared to her even taller and stiller than they had done. She charted each change of direction in her head and saw the pattern of her own progress from a distance, a single, tiny figure in a sea of green.

She had been walking for quite a long time and was beginning to think that she had gone round in a circle. Some animal was calling over to her left with an unfamiliar snorting sound. She thought at first if the worst came to the worst she could call her husband on her mobile. But when she felt in her pocket for its familiar shape she remembered that she had left it in the glove compartment of the car.

She saw a thread on a bush that looked as though it had come from her shirt, the same buff shade, an exact match or as near as you could tell from a single, neutral fibre. Perhaps it was the same fork in the track she had already come to. It seemed to branch at the same angle. And when she crouched down and examined the ground there were what looked like footprints. Whether they were her own was impossible to tell, or even whether they were really footprints. The grass was pushed down, it was true, but they could equally be the tracks of some foraging animal. There was no longer her own for-ward-pointing shadow to orient her. The sun was somewhere else in the sky, hanging on a horizon that she had no access to. If her hus-band were here he would tell her to consider what to do by a process of logical deduction. But she knew with a particular instinct that there was no longer a logic that she could steer herself by.

A light breeze had been blowing in her face since she left the clear-ing. If she kept walking into the breeze, and assuming the wind did not change, she would keep heading in the direction of the road, which ran to the East of the forest, she remembered that from the map. And so she walked directly into the oncoming air, stopping now and then to push back her hair when some unforeseen gust whipped a strand of it across her eyes.

She could not at first believe her senses. If you could hallucinate a smell then that was what was happening to her. Her mouth watered involuntarily and the fine hairs on her arms quivered and lifted. The fire was still smoking slightly in the clearing. The pungent staleness of burnt fish head still lingered in the ash. The mark that her own body had made when she sat on the grass was quite evident to her. A blue sandal that the little girl had been wearing was abandoned next to a rock.

Hallo? She called. Hallo!

But she could tell they had been gone for quite some time. The imperfectly smothered fire was smouldering in token only. Even the residue of laughter had completely disappeared.

She was beginning to feel quite cold and stamped her feet and flapped her arms in an effort to get the blood circulating. She thought now that she might have to spend the night among the trees and did not relish it. Already her flesh was swelling in weals where the midges had bitten her. She went to the stream and knelt down and had a drink of water. In the darkening current her swollen face was barely recognizable.

She sat back on her heels and thought she heard, very faintly from a long way away, a whistle. She shouted, as high as she could manage and got up quickly and clumsily and shouted again. But the piney sound of trees was the only thing that came to her. She decided there was nothing to do but see if she could follow the tracks of the family. She picked up the blue sandal and set off in a direction she had not tried yet, deciphering as best she could the signs of their progress, swinging the blue sandal in her hand.

He arrived back at the car in a state of considerable agitation. He was cold, the flesh on his hands and feet felt desiccated. His throat was dry, he had made himself hoarse by calling his wife's name.

The clock on the dashboard confirmed it was eleven thirty. The arctic twilight, in all its pale luminosity, was settling in on them. He decided he should call for help and got his mobile out but there was no signal.

He walked through the belt of trees and out onto the road, more to check that it was still there than anything, he felt the need to reconnect with civilization. There was no sign of traffic and the road stretched straight and empty in both directions.

He was about to turn back when he heard the thin whine of an engine somewhere in the distance. At first he could see nothing but it sounded as if it was coming from the South. He saw a flash of headlight up against the far trees and then the twin points of light were heading towards him down the straight section. It was coming at speed, nevertheless he stepped out onto the asphalt and waved both his arms in a big arc, and kept on waving. It occurred to him that he looked like a mad man and that no car was likely to stop, but just in the last thirty feet or so the car braked and pulled to a halt beyond him in a cloud of engine fumes.

A man got out and asked him in Norwegian whether anything was the matter.

He did not understand the words but he registered the intonation of enquiry.

My wife, he said. My wife.

He found that he had mislaid her name, he had no other way of referring to her except by the familiar possessive. My wife, he said again. The words came out in a whisper. They had sound to them but, apparently, no heart.

The driver spoke over his shoulder and a woman stepped down from the high interior of the vehicle. Even in the shadows her bright hair had been visible. Now in the extreme twilight the white-blonde substance of it was a shock. She introduced herself, Helle was her name, in quite good English and then, as they got down from the back seats, two children who, she said, were named Mimi and Olaf. Our family, she said with a little laugh. We are on holiday.

She turned away slightly as though at some private observation and it was evident from her outline that another child was very distinctly on the way.

The husband was called Lars, she said. He was tall and bearded and exuded a solid assurance, a bit like an old Norse warrior or some Viking god, as he confirmed that they had indeed seen a woman who fitted the description, yes, it would have been about four hours ago, or six maybe, time was difficult to keep track of in the forest, but it must have been her, the dark hair with a streak of grey in it, the swift, small movements. And it was most unlikely there were two women in beige coloured shirts in the forest simultaneously. Yes, she had seemed relaxed and enjoyed their fish with them. They would go back with him now, they had lights, they were sure to find her. They would take the car for the first part, and sound the horn and stop at intervals. Helle would drive and he and the children would accompany on foot.

I know the paths like the back of my fingers, Lars said. He seemed equally proud of the knowledge and of the idiom.

It could not be very far now until she reached the roadway. She thought intermittently of how re-assuring the gravelled surface would be, clinched into the earth by the hand of man and overriding it, leading from one named place to another, the signs and signatures of the inhabited world.

She had for some time now felt that she was not alone. Each bush, berry-laden and luminous, might conceal something. She was not afraid of it, though it hummed at the edge of where her senses could perceive like an interjection in a conversation that has not taken place yet.

She swung the blue sandal in her hand, to and fro, to and fro, and imagined she could still feel a minute heat from it. She had been walking for hours but was confident now that she was not going round in a circle. Something about the way she was going gave her a conviction of the straight and true. Like an arrow heading for a target she could feel the strength of her own trajectory.

But still the road, which she expected now at every turn, did not appear. She began to suppose that there might not be a road. All her life that she had lived before was in her imagination. There was no husband, no car, no crib, no little lost scraps of pre-humanity. There was only the now, in the whole, rich nothingness of it, and she like a pinnacle.

She stopped, feeling a little breathless. Her own weight felt light, like it never had done. What was this? Expectancy? She caught sight of something up ahead, a sheen or a glimmer, and made her way towards it. The edge of the lake became visible, bearded with reeds and pockmarked all across its surface with lilies. She could not tell what colour the lilies were, perhaps yellow, in this light they looked crepuscular.

She bent down and put her hand in the water, which felt viscous. The lake was no more then a few hundred yards across and looked quite shallow. Where the sun had been on it earlier she could see little spirals of steam. When she saw a movement on the other side it did not surprise her. She knew that it was not an animal, it did not have that furtive confidence. It was human, surely. She could make out the shape of the dress, the cap sleeves with the small, perfect elbows below them, the tendency of the neck. She called out and her voice echoed on the water and came back to her. The child was waving, she could see the quick movement of its hand. Nuala, that was what she had been going to call her own girl. Nuala Faith, and then another name that they had not decided.

The girl was speaking to her now but the words were blurry. She clasped the blue sandal tightly and began walking round the perimeter of the lake. The undergrowth was dense here and the gorse-like bushes scratched at her legs as she pushed through them. She could feel the blood running down into her shoe.

Her progress was slow and it did not look as if the girl was getting any nearer. She stepped into the water and her feet sank into the leaf mould. A few more steps and the water was up to her knees. She could see quite clearly now that the girl had come out onto a spit of land. Just across the water, thirty yards, forty maybe. She waded out, holding the blue sandal up high in her right hand, flexing her free arm out to the left to balance her.

The girl was calling louder now, she could make the words out. Mama. Mama! She did not look, she put one foot in front of the other. She was half way across and the water was up to her waist. It was nothing, she would be there in a moment. The girl had stopped calling and was so close that she could hear her breathing. She listened to the regular breaths with a keen amazement. The bed of the lake rose up and the water receded. She held her hand out, still without looking, and said, I'm here now. It'll be all right.

It was four a.m. the clock on the dashboard said, and the authorities had been out for two hours. They spoke intermittently on walkie-talkies. A helicopter with a heat-seeking device was expected imminently. Lars and Helle had sat with him at first, offering assurances that everything was as it should be. But they had gone now, Helle was very tired with the weight of the baby, and even the children, relatively grown-up though they might be, needed some rest.

It was only a matter of time, he was sure, until they found her. She had huddled down in a hollow in the residual warmth there. She had covered herself with leaves and the softer kind of branches. He thought of her skin, how it felt under his hand when he was making love to her. He thought of his own pleasure and the release that she gave.

He dozed perhaps, he had opted to stay in their own car rather than wait in the police vehicle. He woke up to the smell of her coming off the upholstery. He jerked fully into himself and inhaled her. The light was much stronger now, the sun higher in the sky and the clouds infused with a brilliant luminosity. If he reached out his hand he would surely touch her.

He heard the helicopter somewhere overhead, louder than it had been. There it was, in fact, a black dot punctuating the middle distance. He put his hand to his eyes, there were two helicopters, he wondered a little at the increase in numbers, and wondered too at the bigger grouping of men he saw now gathering around the rescue vehicles.

It didn't bother him much though, why on earth should it? For there she was, his very own wife, coming across the grass towards him. She was not alone. He could see quite clearly that they were all with her. Such clarity. Such detail. The boys looked like her and the girls, perversely, looked like no-one. They were spread out in a line holding hands and she was in the middle of them. He could hear their laughter, see their breath rising in small exhalations. He opened the door of the car and got down and hurried towards them. Joy. Completion! What had he ever done to deserve this? He heard the helicopter engines approaching. They would not be needed. He reached out to greet his family, balancing the sunlight carefully in the palm of his hand.

Miguel's Dream

There is nothing wrong with dreaming, his father had said to him. But you must turn your dreams into reality. This was the basis on which he had built *La Probe Miguel*. It was the basis on which *La Probe* was still dear to him. His father had died several years ago. There was a thumb print in the concrete just next to the *fuenta*. A concrete ring surrounded the *fuenta*, with two brick pillars for the ropes and bucket. It was better than the old arrangement with the iron hoops and the angles. Maybe the thumbprint belonged to his father, there was a certain redoubtable crenelation at the edges. His father, when he came to think of it, had been redoubtable. You could never tell.

They had first driven past *La Probe* together. It was May, as far as he could remember, certainly one of the months before you could begin to see the effects of the dryness. Mostly it didn't rain from April to September. You got droughts here, the region was renowned for it. Down in Malaga they were sometimes worried the tourists would be affected. Things didn't usually get that far up here. But even if they did, *La Probe* wouldn't suffer. It was down in the valley, only a few metres from the river. He had built a swimming pool at the far end of the property which he was proud of. Fourteen metres by seven he said, but they'd dug the hole smaller than he'd wanted. By the time he noticed, the rafting had been sunk and the shape and size were before him. He shouted at the man in charge of the job, who shrugged and lit a cigarillo. We will dig it up again if you want, Miguel, he said. But the house was already taking longer than he'd hoped for. His father was ill and his wife was having a baby. The pool stayed smaller than it should have been, but in his mind it was the size he had always wanted. There was a little difficulty in reconciliation when he swam in it, because his hand came in contact with the tiled edge several strokes before it was due to. But in time he got used to that, and concentrated instead on the irregular shape of the pool which suited its surroundings.

Sometimes when the surface of the water was still you could see a reflection of the mountains. There were mountains on three sides of the property. Their shape was also irregular. If you looked from a plane it was like a grey-white cloth had been caught and ruckled. The countryside was nothing but a high plateau, a respite in the layering of mountains. The valley was a green fault leading to the western border. There were no mountains on the west side. Too far away to see, the land opened out like a shovel. The river got slow there, dragging against its banks. Cadiz and Seville were lowland and did not appeal to him. His dream was part of the upland. He regarded himself very much as an upland man.

He had driven past the property with his father on a clean May morning. The crickets had been particularly noisy the previous night and he was tired. The baby, his little daughter Clara, had been restive. The child Juan that his wife had had two years previously never gave trouble. He would sleep through the very worst of a thunderstorm. But this little one Clara was a different substance. He liked to think she had a wildness he had given her. He liked to think of the seed from his body exploding out into the shape and lineament of her person. But when he thought about it truly he acknowledged the wild side of Clara had probably come from his wife.

That old house of Cerazo's is going to ruin, his father had observed as they drove very slowly past it. The tyres of the battered Subaru rode the ruts easily. The delicate control Miguel exerted through his steering pleased him. Despite being tired, and despite the fact that he no longer desired his wife, there was something very wonderful in being alive. Stop a minute, said his father. Let's take a look at it.

You could get to the door, it looked as though someone still beat a path there. It probably wasn't old Cerazo, the previous winter something had come to him and without saying anything to anyone he'd taken to his bed. The door was held to with a stone, you could easily move it. His father went in, ducking over the step through the broken cobwebs.

The shutters were closed but the sun came in through the cracks and the soft-edged parts where the wood had crumbled. Look at this, his father said, opening a shutter whose latch came off in his hand. Someone should take control of this. It's a good old place. And Miguel, who had a perfectly respectable house on the edge of the town, found himself saying, D'you think he would sell it? He remembered even now how still his father had become. He looked like a shadow by the open shutter, a flat dark cut-out edged by a blaze of light. There's no harm in asking, the voice from the shadow responded. It didn't seem at all like his father, though it had the same sound.

From that day it was a project they shared between them. His wife threw a temper when he told her and said he was mad. We have all we need, Miguel. Who wants other houses? We can put a room on here if need be. She liked living by the town with the people around her. When she looked down into the dark of the valley in the evening she was afraid.

Miguel's father had been a widower since before the marriage. Miguel knew that his wife, who was called Sylvia, was glad that she did not have a mother-in-law. Her own mother lived in a village ten kilometres distant. Sylvia went to visit her twice a week but other than that lived just how she wanted. He would tell her that this or that must happen with the children and she saw to it. But he knew that her women's eye addressed different issues that he had no part of. Within the world that he had she had scooped out a world that he could not access. He did not mind it, but it made her separate from him. It was part of the reason when he reached for her body he had to imagine it was someone else's. He was thirty seven years old and proud of his manhood. There were more difficulties than a man would imagine in marrying and setting up home with a woman as your wife.

The work went on apace once he had negotiated the deal with Cerazo. It was true, perhaps, that he had paid less than the property was worth. Cerazo had always been unworldly, and thought he was getting a good deal. But he had not caught up with the difference in things made by the tourists. People from England particularly wanted property. They would come in the summer and fall in love with some broken down old *finca* with no well and offer the earth for it. It pushed up the prices. Very often they discovered before all the papers were signed that they'd been cheated. Then they withdrew and lost all their money on deposit. It was regrettable, but enough of the contracts went through.

In El Chopo, where the house was that he and his father had driven past, there was a lot of building. From the tangle of apple trees down at the end of the house you could hear the impact of pick and shovel on rock and occasionally the little angry sound of a dumper truck as it went to and fro ridiculously overloaded. But these things were distant, the house was tucked away past the last extremity of the village round a right-hand corner. The river was opposite, and just before it the electricity sub-station with the paint peeling off it and grass growing skyward out of the clogged-up valleys of its roof. The track was rutted and when it rained water gathered there. It took quite a long time for the water to evaporate, and when it did you had to be careful not to sink up to your ankles in mud.

He and his father came every day to monitor progress. His father was good with the men he'd employed to undertake the building. Benito was the foreman, and Alonso and Pepito the two who worked for him. His father made sure all the little things went right, you had to have an eye for detail when building houses. The precise angle of the window reveal was important. The size and shape of the massive oak beams that supported the upper floor were crucial. The ceilings downstairs were open to the wood so any shortcuts or shoddy work-manship would be quickly spotted. What Miguel wanted was everything to be set up in the right relation. Only when one thing was right in relation to the other could there be a sense of peace. I have made sure they pointed that pillar in the way you wanted, his father said to him. With the mortar set back in so the faces of the stones stand out like the parts of a sculpture.

Out of the dark of the interior of the house new shapes grew, all in a single overarching relation that Miguel was aware was his conception. But it was not he who had invented the conception. It was more that the house gave it up to him. At each strike of the hammer, strangely muffled as the walls absorbed it; at each bite of the saw and fall of the wood dust onto the ancient cobbles; at each grunt as a piece of timber was shifted in position – at all of these the house revealed, with painstaking exactitude, the space and substance that was its uniquely. It's coming along pretty well, eh, son? his father asked him. Miguel lit a cigarette and shaded his eyes. The last of the ridge tiles was just being mortared on the roof.

Sylvia was of the opinion that her husband was being unfaithful. She taxed him with it but he denied it. It was quite a usual thing for a man to stray when his wife was expecting a baby, she said. She had hoped better of Miguel, but believed it was impossible to know the man you married. What are you talking about, Sylvia? he said. Your hormones are upset. It is the upset talking. I am busy, I am trying to get the house finished.

He watched as Sylvia drew herself into a globule of bitterness. He told her she must try not to be angry, for the sake of the baby. She pushed her hair back behind her ear and breathed out slowly. Then she said, very quietly so that he hardly heard her, I hate your house.

The quarrel would be mended, Miguel knew that. Such quarrels were part of living with a woman. They got their teeth into something and wouldn't let go until there was an explosion. He worked very hard at the bank in Ronda every morning. He earned good money. In the afternoons instead of a siesta he would work with his partner Paco on one of their systems. They knew that the new technology was where the money was. They had an idea for a system that was worth a fortune. They often worked whole afternoons and then went to the bar.

When a woman has lived any time with a man she develops an instinct for what he is doing. Miguel knew this and it made him uneasy. He had had, for the past eighteen months, a mistress in Ronda. He regarded his period of fidelity to his wife as praiseworthy.

A man can only do his best and he had done it. His wife and his children came first, and always would do. The girl in Ronda, who was a clerk at the bank where he worked, liked the arrangement. She was a modern women with her own interests and looked for discretion. That is what he gave her, along with physical love occasionally on hot afternoons. He did not always work with Paco instead of taking a siesta. The girl had fair hair, quite unlike the dark and rather shortly shorn head of his Sylvia. When he first met her Sylvia's hair had been long, but the heat and the children made her say it was getting in the way and she cut it. He quite liked the look it gave her, like a little boy at certain angles, but at present he liked the long fair hair of his mistress streaked out on the pillow into the shape of a star.

There are as many modes of love as there are modes of people. Miguel was thinking this as he sat in the white plastic picnic chair he had set by the side of the pool. He was looking at the reflection of the mountains in the uncannily flat surface of the water. There was a nearly full moon hanging over the Sierra Madre. That Old Mother, her white teeth, her ashy peaks. He looked into the water and thought, this is like the moon, we are all on the moon. It was one of those occasions when everything is wrong, when you seem entirely out of step with the world your life has created. You feel perhaps like a speck or a bit of leaf. Residue. The house took shape between the fig and the chestnut tree. There was a sound of something falling, a light sound, apple on grass maybe. The apples were very sweet on *La Probe*'s trees, but very often when you took them down the worm had got into them. He would eat his way around the wavy brown line of its tracks very carefully. Really it meant you only ate half an apple. He had long ago decided the best apples were sweet and small.

The house took shape, very solid, very insubstantial. That was how dreams were, as you moved about through them. He got up and walked towards the wall where the gap was that would have the door in it, dark wood and double opening, studded and bolted the way good doors should be. The ground was uneven under his feet, he had just made the previous day with his own hands a path to the pool out of stones that the excavations had dug up. Flat surfaced stones, brownish and grainy. He had not laid them properly as yet, that was his next job, setting the mortar down in a bed underneath them, level-ling them off. In the dark part where the vines hung over, his ankle twisted a little and he swore in a mild, disinterested way. He had felt distant from himself all day, viewing even Sylvia as though she were set far from him, as though she were a little mannequin in whose wooden visage a red mouth moved.

His mistress had told him that morning when he got to work that she was pregnant. She had told him right there in the photocopying room, with the strip-lights over her head making her face seem very white. He could have wished that she had waited and told him at some more appropriate moment, when his arms were around her perhaps and he could feel how warm her flesh was. The photocopier had been churning out sheets of estimates, additions, subtractions, balances, withdrawals. *Kurr*-boom, *kurr*-boom, *kurr*-boom it went, and the contraption at the side moved up and up, collating the paper. It is true, his mistress said, it is true. Her name was Phyllis, he didn't think of it often, but now he saw that 'Phyllis' was what she was, her whole self bounded by the top-heavy 'p', the tall double 'l', the cur-licued 's', interchangeable and endless.

It was indeed true and now Miguel had the taste in his mouth of the truth of it. What did it taste of? It was a bit like dust blown up by a freak wind off the baked ground in high summer. It was sour and gritty. Phyllis had said she would get rid of the child and Miguel was revolted. He had thought of himself as a modern man. He believed (as far as he knew) in phrases like 'the autonomy of the body'. He had never, perhaps, believed in women's rights, but he had believed in the right of women to conduct their own womanly business. Unwanted children had always been got rid of. Tales of it whispered above his head in the oh so easily permeable codes of adulthood – these he could remember, and his mother's face getting smaller as she pursed her lips.

The house was solid under his feet, the new floor had recently been laid, warm terracotta, honey and the palest hint of ailanthus. Even Sylvia had approved. He imagined momentarily his wife's bare feet making their own particular shape on the tiles, how surprisingly compact the little prints would be, damp but then dry again almost immediately. Without being aware that he had done so, he began to cry.

His father had taken to coming to the house every morning. He would arrive before Benito and Alonso and Pepito and leave long after them. Sometimes he would not leave at all, though he had not admitted it. This night he was sleeping in a hammock slung between beams. When he woke up, which he often did in the night, being quite old, he could see the sky through the cracks in the roof where the tiles had not yet been jointed. It was comforting to him, he said, to be able to see so far. You felt you were part of a universe you would not long belong to. Or not in the form that you had, although (he was quite a religious man) no doubt in some other. Being able to see the sky somehow held off dread. He heard the creak of a hinge on a downstairs door, the dry air always made interior metal creaky. He thought at first that his past had come back to haunt him. He thought, particularly when he was afraid, in clichés. But then when he got up and found it was only his son he was disappointed. What brings you here so late at night, Miguel, he said, padding across the terracotta floor in his stockinged feet.

A trouble shared is not necessarily a trouble halved. Sometimes the transmitting of troubles one to another makes them accumulate. The whole world then can seem to be made of trouble. Both father and son were, to differing degrees, aware of this. Nevertheless, something about the shadows and the way the house felt made Miguel tell his father what had occurred that day. As he told him, the light wind that always came up the valley at night rose and fell about the house, smoothing down little abrasions in the gulleys where the rain would go, gaining entry to the kitchen where the women would stand, through a gap where the pipes were to go for the washing machine, there was also to be a dishwasher, the place was to have all mod cons.

Miguel's father heard the wind outside and away to the left in the fig tree. He felt it on the tender flesh at the top of his socks. He knew it well, its sound and precise disposition. It was like a reference point, a needle that swings in a compass, dragging itself north. You know I am not well, Miguel, he said. You know I am dying. Miguel, who had known no such thing, but had felt it deep in his bones like an intimation, nodded. His father was silent for a moment. Even the wind interrupted its small movement in the fig tree. This house must be about the future, not about the past, his father said. And then, against his own will, he went into a past which had always seemed, until that moment, to be distant. He told his son about an event that had happened nearly forty years previously, in that very same house. Of course it was not called *La Probe* then, it was called Rosamaria, after the woman who lived there. Cerazo's wife, that was who she had been, Rosamaria Caballero. She had been very beautiful, at least, then everyone thought so. Nowadays she might not be to everyone's taste. She had had no children, Cerazo being deemed incapable of the act that made them. She looked very separate, moving about her life in a daily way. Miguel's father spoke about how her feet had seemed to move on the cobbles. It was as if, he said, she glided over them. But that, no doubt, was the memory of an old man. He had come there one day about a mule, or maize, and Cerazo had given him beer, and they had sat on a stone step under the part where the vines came over. Rosamaria had come out with a jug. Who can say where love comes from? You do not expect it and then suddenly you turn and look about you and it is there. He had continued for a very long time his liaison with Rosamaria. Cerazo must have known, he turned a blind eye, what man can admit to such fundamental inadequacies?

What had come out of that time, or those times (the old man remembered his hand on Rosamaria's body as though it had been the hand of another) had been a child. It was a little, muling, puking thing, Miguel's father said. If there had been enough light you could have seen that his eyes looked rheumy and the red vein that ran down the side of his nose stood out. He had thought, can this be my child? Rosamaria had had it in a town many miles away at the house of her sister. He remembered the wild look on her face as she sat up in bed. And what happened to the child? Miguel asked. He had lit three cigarettes in the course of the story and they had all gone out. He is sitting beside me, the old man answered. It was very quiet in the moments after he had spoken. Not even an owl went by.

The next day Miguel resolved to tell his wife of his predicament. Perhaps she can go and speak to Phyllis, he thought, keeping not quite careful enough a watch as he shaved, nicking the corner of his mouth where a spot was forming, watching the blood run down. Perhaps she can offer to take the child. That he had made two women pregnant simultaneously, vaguely occurred to him. It was an unfortunate predicament for a man. However, he wanted both his children. The matter seemed relatively simple when you thought about it. He would pay Phyllis to have the child. Then he and his wife would bring it up as their own. If only the conceptions had been a little closer! They could always have made out, for public consumption, that Sylvia had had twins.

It did not work out as simply as Miguel had expected. When he told his wife she threw a tantrum and broke their most precious jug over his head. She took the two children and slowly, painfully now, her stomach was very large and heavy, got into the car. She had insisted he drove her to her mother's. She needed to get away from him for a few days and think.

When he went into the bank on the Thursday after staying away there was no Phyllis. He walked past her desk at the farthest corner of the second floor and its surface was paperless. Not even one of the pale blue clips that she put round folders was there to betray her. Miguel thought suddenly, we will have a son. At the same time he felt slightly sick, as you do with a shock or when someone has hit you. Where is Phyllis? he asked the secretary. We have an important project to discuss. But did you not know, Miguel? Phyllis is taking a holiday this week. She has gone to Madrid to visit her cousin Fernanda. She is going to the Prado and said she will shop till she drops.

Miguel felt something like a panic take hold of him. To keep it at bay he immediately resolved that he would follow Phyllis to Madrid. He did not know where she could have gone. He asked the secretary for her address there but she did not have it. He tried her later by email but received no reply. He made some excuse at the office and left early, determined to go home and pack, and drive to Madrid overnight. He telephoned and left a message with his wife's mother that business with Pablo had taken him away, but that he would be back on Sunday. His wife would not speak to him, and the tone of voice of his mother-in-law was cold.

At his house the air was stuffy, it was unusual that no door or window had been opened during the day. The silence too that was generated by the absence of his family bore down on him. He packed what was necessary to get him through two days in a big city like Madrid, and locked the door behind him. One of his neighbours, a man called Manolo who had recently moved there, waved at him and called out Hola!

Miguel drove down into the valley which was out of his way, but it was necessary to tell his father where he was going. All the way down through the bends, past where the olives had burnt last year where a careless driver had thrown out his cigarette, past the ruined house that no-one had bought because it was too near the road, past the fancy new place that some people from Cadiz had built and put on ignominious gold turrets, past the pool of Juan Carlos with his little girl swimming and the water in a pale green tide slapping over the edge, down and down again he went, into the valley with the light almost gone (so it looked from the top) and nearer and nearer *La Probe* came, he could see the shape the roof made, deeply shadowed in the crenellations of its tiles, close under the apple trees.

The gravel made a spitting sound under the tyres as the car halted. Father, he called, it's Miguel. The old man seemed to be hiding. The door was ajar, he tended to shut it last thing at night, about eleven. He had taken to sleeping there all the time. He said it suited him. Miguel walked around the pool and saw the moon beginning to rise in its flat surface. He said, Papa? just as he had when he was a child. It was only slightly surprising to find the old man in the chair by the door, just inside, by the closed window. It was evident from the first instant that he was dead. He had died, so it looked, soon after the builders left, unless they went early, hearing no sound and thinking he had fallen asleep. He was cold but not set, and looked sad and a little puzzled. Miguel tidied his hands in his lap and wondered if he had been aware, and what he had been thinking. Outside (it seemed blasphemous to do it indoors with his father there) he called up his wife. Reception was bad, he had to move off a few yards from the house with his phone to his ear.

By the time his father was buried Phyllis had come back. She was looking thinner, whip-thin in fact, her face was drawn down around her cheekbones – and her hair, surely it was duller and lanker than it had been previously? She confirmed she'd dealt with the matter of the pregnancy there in Madrid. It was quick, it was easy, in a manner of speaking. He offered to pay for what she had done, but she smiled and refused him.

I'm sorry, he said. So sorry, Phyllis.

She shrugged and said, There's no need to be sorry, Miguel. These things happen. That's life.

His wife had her baby two months later and they called him Miguel. With surprisingly little difficulty he persuaded his wife to move down to *La Probe*. It seemed that life on the edge of the town no longer satisfied her. She said little these days, watching the babies grow.

Miguel's work in the bank did not get him as far as he'd hoped and Paco moved off to another project in Barcelona. Phyllis too had gone to live in another town. He found time on his hands in the summer evenings. He opened his laptop with less enthusiasm than he used to. Try as he might he could not remove the picture of Phyllis's smile from his mind.

La Probe was the one thing that gave him satisfaction. The house was exactly as he had foreseen it. He swam every morning in the pool whose size he often boasted of. You must turn your dream into reality, his father had said.

He sat in the chair that had been designated his between pool and apple trees and watched the Old Mother grow spiky in the twilight.

Come here, he called to Clara, who was waiting on tiptoe in the doorway as she did each evening. She had the little one Miguel by the hand, he was walking already, and together they staggered towards him over the grass.

Miguel has a present, Clara said, and the little boy handed him a windfall apple, very rotten and pockmarked. He could see quite clearly the little, brown pucker where the worm had entered.

Eyes so much like mine, he thought, looking at the boy, as the chill air from the Sierra Madre fell down over them.

His wife appeared at the kitchen doorway, shading her eyes against the evening light, which was flat and piercing. That morning she had told him she was expecting again.

Why are you looking so surprised? She'd asked him. Like some silly teenager. It was you. It was me. Actions have consequences.

Are you coming in, Miguel? She called to him now. It's getting cold. We don't want you coming down with the ague. The man of the house. There's the family to think of.

Clara was looking expectantly at the apple in his hand and his son was clawing at his trouser legs, beginning to whimper.

Are you going to eat it, Papa? The girl asked.

It looked as though Sylvia was laughing, he could not be sure.

Without any more thought he bit hard into the apple flesh, swallowed it whole, finished it down to the core in two bites. He imagined the worm wriggling its way down into his gut, aperture by aperture.

Bravo Miguel, his wife called out now. Bravo, handled like a true man.

She was laughing, he could see the way her body shook, her shape in the doorway thickening already.

He scooped up his son over his shoulder and took Clara's hand.

I'm coming, Sylvia, I'm coming, he said.

By the time he got to the door she'd gone in. He paused on the threshold. It was still light outside, with that peculiar intensity you get just when dark is about to fall.

What are you waiting for Daddy? Clara asked.

I don't know, he said. I don't know, Clara.

Then he heard himself laughing, loud and deep, a real belly laugh, like a man he had known once who lived in a different country, very far away.

A CALM NIGHT OVER THE ATLANTIC

The take-off out of Dulles late last night was bumpy. I'd had a gin too many in the Club lounge and a queasy feeling had settled onto my gut. When they called the flight my stress-levels jumped because it was 803, the same number as the one that crashed in Pennsylvania, instead of going on to the Pentagon.

It was slow going through baggage screening and the ground attendants all looked like they were frowning. There was a man in front of me with a big moustache. He looked a little like Friedrich Nietzsche. I had a book by Nietzsche in my hand baggage. I'm writing on him for a Sunday Supplement.

As we go through the gate there's a little red light that keeps on blinking. A Latin-looking woman has a bulky ground phone up to her ear. I focus on staying calm and practice breathing. Slow and steady. That's how you do it. I first got nervous when they blew the Beirut flight out of the sky over Tripoli. They blew the side out and six people got sucked out, seats and all, their drinks and their little plastic trays and their in-flight magazines all plucked out at thirty two thousand feet. Imagine that. I hope they didn't know what hit them. Thirty two thousand feet is six miles. That's an awful long way till you hit the ground.

I always read on planes, and never bother with the in-flight entertainment. Exterminator Ten or the latest Harry Potter doesn't draw me. I knew already what was on the news channel. I'd seen it on the screens in the Club Lounge. A building blowing up in Basra. An awful lot of dust and stuff, arms and legs all going off in different directions, and then something round, a head or something, coming towards you like a soccer ball.

The attendant gives me a drink and says, Looks like you're in for a good read, nodding at my Nietzsche. The cover is a painting. I don't know paintings. Or at least I know some, the great big landscapes, the prairies with the dust clouds coming up at the edges of them, the covered waggons. The ball of tumbleweed. That wide open early American art you get in the Phillips. That's what I like. Whenever I'm in Washington I take the afternoon and go there. When you stand in front of those great big landscapes you feel like you're standing on the edge of the world.

The cover on the Nietzsche book is different. It's mostly half clad nymphs with garlands round their heads being pursued by Satyrs. You can just see the dark hooves sticking out here and there, like a clip from an internet porn cam. The Satyrs are being attended by curly headed cherubs with wicked expressions. They're offering beverage of some kind, mead, wine, whatever golden intoxicant they'd have had in Arcadia. The satyrs have little horns and one of them has his arms cut off, like in a statue.

I can see the lights go by, slowly at first as we taxi. Then everything holds still while we wait at the end of the runway for our slot. The captain comes on and says, don't worry about anything. We'll be fine. It's a calm night over the Atlantic.

The runways are getting longer these days, that's how I feel it. Then we're up at last with that lurch of weightlessness that blows your mind.

I've lived in England for ten years now, though it seems more recent. Those cute little dinky fields, I'll never get over the first time I saw them. Under the wingtips of the plane they came up. It was early morning. What peace, I thought, what history, what order! I got my paper to send me over as their correspondent. I knew once they'd sent me that things would never be the same.

Since then I've had two homes so, as I generally say, my home is nowhere. There was a guy in some book or other that turned it round into EREHWON. I like Erehwon, I like the idea of it, but no one back home in the States ever gets it. Back home in England they think I'm kinda strange to keep going on about it. My wife cocks her head on one side when we give dinners and says, It's his hobby horse, my poor, dear, husband. It's just one of those *things* about the Yew-Knighted-States.

Across the aisle, to the right, is a solitary woman. I can only see her in profile, she's staring straight ahead. She has a white shirt on, and something soft and dark draped over it. Her hands are very white in her lap and the nails are painted.

She looks across and she has grey eyes which I find surprises me. I remember a phrase from somewhere: 'It is easy to be surprised in these days'. There's going to be quite a wait till dinner because there's a storm up ahead and there'll be turbulence. I say to the flight attendant, Can't we go round it? She smiles that smile and says, It's a big one. And then she offers me a second cocktail by way of a consolation. I order Jack Daniels, on the rocks, no twist, and when she brings it I tilt the seat back and get ready to read.

I didn't expect it to be easy reading, this Nietzsche. I'm an experienced reader, I took a liberal arts degree from Saskatchewan State. I'm pretty much in to most things current. Of course, the Europeans are different. I know that. I can see from the way they've tended to react to things. I've had to keep quiet a lot, recently, in bars and suchlike, with my friends and acquaintances. London isn't what it was, I have to say it. And I don't feel the same kind of welcome when I'm in Paris and walking down the Grands Boulevards.

They'll catch up with us, that's what my dad would have said. He was in trash cans, made a lot out of it. I learned a lot from him. Mostly what I learned was about staying grounded. You just keep your eye on the ball, Son, he said. That's what'll get you places. And it has. His own dad was a second generation immigrant. The old man came over on a boat around eighteen ninety. From one of these weird places east of the Danube. Maybe it was Serbia. You get so you can't keep up with it, all these changes. I think I liked the cold war It gave you security.

So: Nietzsche is a nihilist. That's OK. You don't believe in anything. But as I read on I think, hang on, this guy is different. This is a guy who Believes. In. Nothing. Can you get this? Does it make sense to you? I believe in – well. I believe in Life. And the Flag. I believe in neat-cut yards, and putting your trash out. I believe in pumpkins by the side of the road in October. I believe in my wife, in my nice, English wife that I married ten years ago. Although sometimes I think I don't know her. Sometimes I wonder if you can like someone you don't know.

It's the *Selected Nietzsche,* that's the book I'm reading. I can feel the woman across the aisle looking at the cover. I look up. She's tapping the red nails on the arm of her seat.

Good book? She says.

I nod.

Good enough.

She looks like she's going to say something else but she doesn't. The soft, dark stuff of her wrap has slipped down, I can see the line of her shoulder where it meets her hair.

I tell her I'm a writer and reading this for an assignment. Apparently, she writes too.

Just in a small way of course, she says, laughing a little. She's a widow, and retracing the trip she took with her husband seventeen years ago for their honeymoon.

Sentimental, I know, she says, but, well, somehow I just knew it was me, and I had to.

There's nothing, I say, like a trip down Memory Lane.

The seat belt signs have been off for a while but there's still no dinner. Apparently there's some more turbulence up ahead.

D'you think it's turbulence, she says, or could it be really – you know – *Something?*

I don't know, I say. And then she says,

Sorry, sorry. I get like this since my husband's – . I told you that he died.

You did, I say. The fan dividers on the other seats are pulled forward. The lights are down lower than normal. It feels like we're alone.

You shouldn't be crying, I say. Here, have this. I give her my handkerchief. There's nothing to cry about.

But there is.

And then she tells me. Her husband was one of the three thousand, eight hundred and forty two that perished. He was up in the left hand tower. Up high, high, with the greatest view over Manhattan. That view, he would say to her sometimes. It stands for something. It's what keeps us alive. He came down the stairs. He was half way down when it all gave way. The concrete bubbled and swelled and the metal melted. Down into all that he went, and burned up. That's as near as she can figure.

He was in accountancy, she said. He worked with numbers. And now he's become one. Just a number. One of the ones.

I reach out and put my hand on her wrist. It's a long way to reach, over the aisle in Club class. Her skin is surprisingly warm. It seems to calm her.

I'm sorry, she says. I'm sorry.

Right there flying over the Atlantic with Newfoundland down to the left I become very English. I pat her wrist and say, Not at all. Not at all.

There's something Nietzsche says that has really got me. Happiness, he says *is the feeling that power is growing, that resistance is being overcome.* I know *I* feel happy when that's happening. When you're breaking through and making something happen that you want to.

I think about this as the plane drives on. Just like your own living room but bigger. Kind of suspended. A nowhere between nowheres. The will to power, that's what he calls it. But it seems to me just like getting from A to B, like we all do. And what's wrong with that? You win some. You lose some. He says that pity holds you back, it's like a contagion. I think I've felt pity. I believe so. But then I think, really? When did I? And I honestly don't know. Did I pity those people at the top of the tower holding hands and jumping? I think I remember I saw them falling like leaves.

I do feel something now, and it isn't pity. It's something I haven't felt for a long time. I've tried not to feel it because married men don't, that's what my dad said. When you feel it, son, turn away and think of your wife, he said to me. I do try to think of my wife, but instead of her what I see is the grey eyes of the woman across from me. I look up, and there she is, looking at me like she knows what I'm thinking.

Do you ever get lonely on a flight? I ask.

I get lonely lots of places, is what she says to me. I get lonely at home. In my car. At the store. I get lonely sitting. Standing. Walking. Breathing.

Are you lonely now?

I'm very lonely.

So am I.

And I realize then it's absolutely true. I'm lonely as hell. I'm living now and I'll be dead one day. That's it. That's all.

Let's go somewhere and talk, is what I say.

Most people are snoozing or glued to their screens with that manic stare that gives me the willies. No sign of cabin crew. It could be a ghost-ship or rocket of zombies headed for outer space.

We push past the curtains and find a little, secluded space next to an exit and a galley that isn't being used tonight. There's just one lavatory at the far side but no one's in need of the facilities right now.

Here we are, she says.

She's looking pretty shy, and older in the light here than I originally thought her.

I'm feeling a bit like a kid, I say to her.

Me too. She smiles, and her teeth are crooked.

I haven't been alone with a man, other than my husband, for thirty years.

Can I kiss you? I say. I have an idea you're supposed to ask about such things these days.

She doesn't say yes, but she doesn't need to. And my god, how she tastes – the sweetness of it is indescribable.

This is crazy, isn't it?

The whole world's crazy.

You're married, I suppose?

I am. I was.

And I realize then that I don't know what any of it means, the forms, the structures. I can't bring my wife to mind or see her anywhere in my head. There's nothing but this. The here and now. It's what I've been waiting for all my life. Cut loose. Cut free.

There's no need to speak, we're already heading for the little red light that says 'Washroom', and below it, the blue door.

I don't know her. I don't need to. I know with my heart and my gut and my soul.

This is living, I think, with my hand reaching out to the blue door, the tip of my fingers on the latch already. And I see in this instant that dying doesn't matter anymore. This is all. This is everything.

And all I know is, the wrap on her shoulder is slipping down and you can practically see through her shirt and something comes over me, god, I can hardly wait till we get through that blue door, I want to do it right there, on the floor, with only a skin of metal between us and the thin air, that thin gold dawn up ahead of us. I put out my hand to steady her, and the plane gives a lurch and she's right up against me, I can smell her and feel her. She breathes on my cheek and the taste of her, sweet and then bitter, gets into my head.

The seat signs ping on and the chief steward's voice booms out just above us. Before he can say two words there's a loud bang and what I see through the exit porthole is a bolt of flame coming out of the side of the plane and heading for the wingtip. Someone screams, just a few seats beyond the closed curtain, and I think, this is it. Something happens, a clenching and a letting go, and I can feel I've wet myself. It's quiet, eerie, a vast silence in the seats and walkways. But the engines keep turning, the plane keeps climbing, time goes on laying its tracks out, slow and then fast.

I've gone cold, icy cold. So has she. We go back though, unsteadily, like drunks. My legs are trembling. I handle her into the seat, then slide back into mine, my hands and my ankles are shaking, there's a gale from space that's set up an airway inside me. The cabin staff top up the drinks more swiftly than usual. It is only the hand of God, only some lightning. I think about what it would be like to be falling, down in a great big spiral out of the sky.

I look at the woman just one more time in the whole of the flight and she looks back at me. We're strangers, total strangers. I intend to say goodbye when we land, just out of politeness, but she disappears while I'm getting my bags down.

My wife is waiting at the barrier to meet me. We touch lips briefly. How was the flight? She says.

Not bad, I say. I didn't sleep. I read quite a lot of Nietzsche.

Nietzsche? She says. She's looking at something behind me, over my shoulder. Then, taking charge like always, she says, here, let me have that bag.

Would you like a swim? She says. Or go straight home?

Let's go home, I say.

The roundabouts come in their familiar sequence. Shepherd's Bush. The Westway. Then we're in the well heeled streets of our neighbourhood.

Marco Pierre White has opened a new restaurant, she says, Shall we go this evening?

I don't think so, I say.

The sky is relatively clear for the time of year, and high up above us I can see the track of a jet engine and there at the tip of it the silver arrow of a plane ascending.

Where would you like to go, then? My wife says.

From the side for an instant she looks like one of the nymphs in the painting.

I press the electric button and let down the window. London comes in at me. I hear a clock chiming, Big Ben maybe.

Nowhere, I say. Nowhere. That's where I'd like to go.

5. SOMEWHERE

Furious Interiors

(Fragment of an Agon)

Ghosts live in rooms, whether in houses or in the head too. Ghosts live in words and in silences lying just behind the words. Ghosts live in books, in the lines on the page, in the spaces, the margins, the spine, the stitching, in the pause and the dash and the question mark. And of course, ghosts live most of all in every full stop.

It's a warm, sunny day, as warm as you get in the hills in the West. Not a breath of wind. Nothing stirring at all. In the stone sitting room of a medieval house, Perth y Felin is its name, I am sweeping the hearth. The hearth is an inglenook fireplace you can walk right into. Nine feet wide by five feet high by four feet deep. Flagstones. A bread oven set into the wall behind, on the left. Old metal hooks where the animals hung after slaughter to be smoked. A cranking machine that turned over the pig when it went to be roasted. I bend forward with a dustpan and brush in my hand to clear up some ash from a log that's fallen the previous evening. Even in summer you need a fire there as the nights draw down. The walls are rock and three feet thick. The chimney is open at the top to the sky. I have sometimes thought a star might fall down and land in the fireplace.

I am sweeping, it is ordinary, the sun is out. I can see through the window benign-looking fields and a few sheep grazing. As I bend forward something icy descends on the back of my neck. I don't know what's happening and stop, stock still. I can feel my hair beginning to lift away from my scalp – standing on end – and my arms and my legs, every hair in its follicle. The chill is extreme and with it comes suddenly an absolute instinct that I must get away. I drop the dustpan and brush on the floor, race out of that fireplace, out of that room, away from the icy fingering that has suddenly touched me, into the sun and the day and the life. Normality. The real world. Everything in an instant gone back to how it should be.

But not quite. Not ever. For the rest of the day I go about my business as usual. Except, I do not go near that corner of the fireplace. My partner steps in and brushes it up and makes a joke. He is nothing if not a practical man.

That evening I look up on the internet 'hair standing on end', 'cold on the back of the neck' and so on. I find I am one of many people who have experienced these phenomena. I find that this is the classic, staple, manifestation of an apparition. From that moment I understand that this ancient house I live in is haunted. Why should it not be? Five hundred years of lives and deaths there. From that moment onwards I know for certain there are ghosts.

There are no attics at Perth y Felin for the bedrooms are tucked up under the roof in what would have been once the store place for grain. There's been a house there – or a dwelling at least – since thirteen hundred. The oldest room, whose wall is a higgledy-piggledy mess of rock and infill is from fifteen hundred. Civilization, you might say, or at least the beginnings of a certain affluence, date from the sitting room at sixteen forty. Then pieces were added, this room, that room. The roof, once sod, was slated – God knows when. Then more recently – in the nineteenth century? In the twentieth century? There's no one alive who knows that now – the lath and the battens and the purlins and the slates were raised on one side and dormers constructed. Light in the attics! Bedrooms. Modernity. Except when you're lying up under that roof, in the night, in the storms that come in from the West with intense regularity, you know that modernity is a paper-thin construct. You listen to the mice scuttering in the rafters just inches away from where you are resting. The bats in the eaves, shifting and scratching. The house creaks as the rocks in the walls ease then restabilize.

I have been in this house for thirty years. If thirty years is a generation then twenty generations of people have lived here. My father lived to be nearly a hundred so if we take his lifespan to be a measurement, this house has been occupied for just seven life spans. Someone said to me recently, with that calculation, there are only twenty people between me and Christ.

The attics, before they became bedrooms, were grain stores. For this place was a mill and as such was the heart of the local community. The grain in the attics, bulging and pungent. The water wheel turning. The flour being milled and ground and deposited there in its creamy dryness in wooden containers. The smell of baked bread. When we pulled down the ceiling and put in a new one thirty years ago the grain fell in clusters. Veritable little snowstorms of grain from this corner, that crevice. I picked it up in dry little handfuls and let the chaff fall through my open fingers. Now it still falls but singly, occasionally. In what year did they harvest that singular grain? Under what mode of thresher did the sheaf fall? I put out my hand to catch a grain as it falls through the sunlight. If ghosts had voices I would ask these questions of the ghost that lives here, for she must know this, she must know everything.

Sometimes I half expect the grain to be snatched away by an unseen hand as I reach towards it. That hasn't happened yet. There's silence and the merest flit of something as the light changes. Somewhere away at the end of the house a door clicks to and fro on its hinges. This is what time is. The door on the hinge that you can never go through. The promise of something that will never, ever be fulfilled.

ACKNOWLEDGEMENTS

Acknowledgements are due to the editors of the following publications where some of these stories first appeared. 'Thiruvega' was published in *Words and Women* prizewinners' anthology (Unthank Press). 'The Returning' appeared in *Wired to the Dynamo* (Cinnamon Press, ed. Matthew Jarvis). 'Heritage Road' was broadcast on BBC Radio 4. 'The Little Lost Ones' was published in Collection of Wales Short Stories in Tamil titled *THERNTHEDUTHA WALES SIRUGA-THAIGAL* (Short Fiction from Wales), Kalachuvadu Publications.

THE AUTHOR

Clare Morgan is a fiction writer and literary critic who lives in Gwynedd and Oxford. Her novel *A Book for All and None* was published by Weidenfeld & Nicolson and her short story collection, *An Affair of the Heart*, by Seren. Her stories have been widely anthologized, and broadcast on BBC Radio 4. Her book *What Poetry Brings to Business* was published by University of Michigan Press and her recent writing on the subject has featured in the *Wall Street Journal*, *FastCompany*, and *Humanizing Business: What Humanities can say to Business*. She is founder and director of Oxford University's creative writing degree, and a Fellow of Kellogg College, Oxford.

An Affair of the Heart

Each story in *An Affair of the Heart* questions the apparently romantic title through its exploration of the enigmatic state of mind known as love. Desire and identity; displacement, emotional and geographical; the relationship between ambition, circumstances and emotion; the sometimes difficult co-existence of passion and intellect; these are the subjects of the fifteen fascinating narratives.

Men and women reckon the worth of relationships past and present, from steamy New Orleans to urbane Paris, from metropolitan Chelsea to the industrial valleys and rural hinterlands of Wales. Frank and delicate, revelatory and secret, Morgan's stories offer insights into human nature which are by turns punchily realistic and evocatively questioning.

www.serenbooks.com

PRAISE FOR CLARE MORGAN

A Book for All and None

This novel of love, madness and creativity is written with eloquence and artistry. – *Mail on Sunday*

Stuffed to bursting with good things … Past and present are very neatly plaited together. – *The Times*

Morgan manages that symphonic trick of weaving her parallel narratives into a spell-binding, effortlessly propulsive unity. – *Independent*

Woven into this ambitious brainteaser of a novel is the beginning of Nietzsche's intense, obsessive relationship with Louise von Salomé in 1882, Woolf's Pembrokeshire sojourn of 1908, and the origins of her first book … it is unashamedly intellectual and sensually written. – *Guardian*

Morgan … masters her disparate materials impressively … [the] novel unfolds like a work of paper-sharp origami to reveal its incredible secret. – *Times Literary Supplement*

A beautiful, haunting literary novel from an extraordinary talent … Looking at the lives of two academics through their passions for the philosopher Nietzsche and novelist Virginia Woolf, *A Book for All and None*, is highly accessible and thought provoking. – *Lovereading Novel of the Month*

An Affair of the Heart

Far from the romantic collection the title suggests, Clare Morgan's book of short stories, *An Affair of the Heart*, is an often uncomfortable look at love and desire in their many forms. No living happily ever after here. These stories mix the wonderfully everyday – a father pulling on a potentially ill-fitting sock watched by his daughter – with the unbearable – a furtively glimpsed view of domestic violence.

Morgan … is clearly a writer who has honed her art, comfortable with using the short story as a way to explore some of life's more complex themes. Read her collection to have notions of love, desire and relationships challenged, not to enjoy a cosy evening on the sofa with a box of chocolates … These are savoury tid-bits, for a palette used to strong flavours. – *Michael Nobbs www.gwales.com*

What Poetry Brings to Business

Morgan, Oxford University director of creative writing, tackles the false opposition between art and commerce in this thorough and thoughtful attempt at making poetry accessible—even necessary—to businesspeople. Through a liberal application of her favorite poems, Morgan argues that the act of reading poetry changes the way the reader thinks, that bare facts are not enough to elicit good business decisions, and that the act of poetic deconstruction helps develop skills that are applicable to business. She speaks passionately about strategies of creativity and how poems bridge the gap between knowing and perceiving because they use the highly differentiated, logic-driven structures of language to point to the undifferentiated area where emotions hold sway. – *Publishers Weekly*

At last there is a book that explores the deep but unexpected connections between business and poetry. Clare Morgan … demonstrates how the creative energy, emotional power, and communicative complexity of poetry relate directly to the practical needs … that face business managers. There has never been a book on developing managerial potential quite like this one. – *Dana Gioia*